The M*atrix*

JONATHAN AYCLIFFE

HarperPaperbacks
A Division of HarperCollinsPublishers

This is a work of fiction. The characters, incidents, and dialogues are products of the author's imagination and are not to be construed as real. Any resemblance to actual events or persons, living or dead, is entirely coincidental.

HarperPaperbacks *A Division of* HarperCollins*Publishers*
10 East 53rd Street, New York, N.Y. 10022

Cover illustration by Gerry Grace

First printing: June 1995

Printed in the United States of America

HarperPaperbacks and colophon are trademarks of HarperCollins*Publishers*

❖ 10 9 8 7 6 5 4 3 2 1

THERE IS NO ESCAPE FROM
THE CORE OF EVIL

I slammed the book shut and sat back, stupefied by the obscenity of the woodcut I had happened on. One thing I knew with absolute certainty—and I know it now without any hint of doubt—whoever the artist was who had penned that loathsome scene had not imagined it, but had drawn it from life.

As I sat there, glancing nervously about me, I became aware for the first time that there were noises in the room above me. Something told me that they had been there for some time, but engrossed as I had been in my reading, I had failed to notice them. I strove to make out what they could be. A sort of flapping and scraping that moved slowly across the floor above my head. At first I thought it must be a member of the Fraternity who had come to investigate the lights, or perhaps, the apartment upstairs had been rented without my knowledge.

But even as I listened, something in the quality of the sounds told me that, whatever was making them, it was not human. My heart seemed to freeze as the noises moved across the room in the direction of the door that led to the first-floor landing. I heard the door opening, and the sound moving across the wooden floor. Terrified, I went to the door of the library. Somewhere above me, I could hear it, very soft, like seaweed on damp rocks, flapping and wriggling across the landing.

As I stood listening, it reached the first step and started down the stairs.

Books by Jonathan Aycliffe

The Matrix
The Vanishment
Whispers in the Dark
Naomi's Room

Writing as Daniel Easterman

The Ninth Buddha
Brotherhood of the Tomb
Night of the Seventh Darkness
Name of the Beast
The Judas Testament

Available from HarperPaperbacks

To Beth:
With fond memories of my last year in Edinburgh

Acknowledgments

My thanks as always, but with undimmed enthusiasm, to my editor, Patricia Parkin, for the subtle and intelligent deployment of her skills; to Mary-Rose Doherty for her incisive and informed copy-editing; and to my wife Beth, for enjoying the stories, and for being there.

Who is the third who walks beside you?
When I count, there are only you and I together
But when I look ahead up the white road
There is always another one walking beside you
Gliding wrapt in a brown mantle, hooded . . .

T. S. Eliot: *The Waste Land*

'S an fhàsach iad air seachran chaidh
an ionad falamh fàs;
Is bail' air bith cha d'fhuaradh leo
gu còmhnuidh ann no tàmh.

Psalm 107:4

Chapter 1

EVEN NOW, IT SEEMS STRANGE to me that I should be writing this memoir at all. With every day and every week that passes, the whole experience takes on an air of unreality. For a moment, dark wings seem to fold about me, then there is a flutter and they are gone, and the air is clear as if they had never been. And then I listen, and the silence is silence no longer. There are sounds, familiar sounds, sounds that have no right to be there.

My rational side tells me that it was nothing more than the work of my imagination. But then I pause, transfixed by the contradiction: I am not an imaginative man. Quite the reverse. There are those who might say my powers of inventiveness atrophied in late childhood. I am an academic, a sociologist, a late-twentieth-century man of reason, not a dreamer. My approach to the phenomena I study is, as far as possible, that of a scientist: in preparing papers, I take care to censor out anything that seems colored by personal bias or fancy, anything that derives from speculation rather than tested and testable evidence.

Was that a sound just now? I thought . . . Well, let us say . . . I will admit that I do still hear things from time to time, things no one should hear. They are in my imagination, nowhere else. If not . . .

How can it be that someone like myself, a rational man, is haunted by these nightmares, pursued in the dark hours before dawn by specters only the most fevered imagination could create? Even in broad daylight I have been startled by sudden shadows thrown across a patch of sunlight over grass, and out of the corner of my eye I have caught sight of curious shapes scuttling away. My reason denies it, my reading and learning dismiss it; but I have seen things that I dare not think about when I am alone. There are sounds which, if I were to hear them again, would, I think, drive me mad.

I must be more systematic. If this story is to be told and if I am to attempt an analysis of what I believe I experienced, I must tackle the subject as I would any case history. In distancing myself from events, I shall make my readers better able to evaluate what they read and give myself a better opportunity to come to terms with my own experiences. If, at times, I do not always succeed in preserving a detached and scientific style, you must forgive me. It is just that . . . these things are very fresh. And I think it is not over yet, that these days without the darkness are just a lull.

My name is Andrew Macleod. I am thirty-three years old, having been born on the 15th of July 1961. My father's name was Calum, my mother's Margaret. I am an only child, without brothers or sisters. My father before me was an only child, and his father before that. I understand isolation, I do not fear solitude. Or I did not until these things began.

More facts. I shall set down all the facts, so that you will know none of this is imagination, that I see and hear and think as well and as soundly as you. The facts are what separate us from children and savages. They are our best defense against our innate proneness to exaggerate and fantasize. What you will read here, I assure you, shall be only facts, as far as I know them.

I was born on Lewis, the eastern half of the island of Harris and Lewis in the Outer Hebrides. My father taught Gaelic in the secondary school in Stornoway, although he was originally a mainlander from Inverness. He had met my mother, a Lewis woman, while living in Stornoway during a summer vacation from Aberdeen University, where he was studying Gaelic and Irish; they married soon after he took his degree, and he stayed in Stornoway to teach.

It took the natives a long time to accept him. Mainland Scots are foreigners to the islanders, and it did not go down well at first that he had come to teach their children what they held to be their own language. In the end, however, his command of the tongue and of the literature in it, as well as his personal popularity with his pupils, won them over. In time, he occupied an honored place in Stornoway society.

My upbringing was marked by a curious blend of my father's skepticism and my mother's simple faith. As a child, I went with her to church every Sunday. On Lewis, the Free Church of Scotland—the Wee Free as it is popularly known—was the dominant sect, in stark contrast to the Catholicism of Uist to the south. The sparseness of the church building, the Calvinistic fervor of the sermons, and the black clothes worn by both men and women remain to this day etched in my memory.

But it is the singing that haunts my deepest dreams and echoes behind and ahead of me. No one who has not heard it can imagine the eerie sound of that singing, the mournful incantation of the Gaelic metrical psalms. A precentor chants each line in turn and is followed by the congregation in a low, lilting wave of sound, a disharmony of separate voices that achieves its own harmony in the rising and falling of the words as they bind them together. There is no musical accompaniment, no organ, no harpsichord, just the lonely sound of the chanting voices and, in the long dark winters, the cruel wind keening outside, with the desolation of the vast northern seas in it. It is the music of a people born among mists and endless storms, close to the sea and death.

I did well at school and, with my father, traveled several times to the mainland in my teens. Once we all went to London for an entire week.

The great city frightened me with its size and bustle; yet it drew me with the promise of unexplored possibilities. I dreamed of its streets and high, many-windowed buildings long after I returned to my island. On a street map I would trace with a mesmerized finger the routes we had taken to the sights, seeing them all again in my mind's eye: the Houses of Parliament, the Tower, St. Paul's, Harrods. There had been more things in that one shop than in all the shops and houses of Harris and Lewis put together.

My father was called on frequently to travel to spots in the Inner and Outer Hebrides, to visit schools, to talk to local institutes, and to consult with colleagues. I sometimes went with him, to North and South Uist, Benbecula, and Barra in a small boat sailed by a local fisherman. On other occasions, we went by McBrayne's steamer past Skye and the Kyle of Lochalsh, to Mallaig on the west coast of the mainland. The train between Mallaig and Fort William was the first I ever saw.

I shall always remember the last time we made the journey back from Mallaig to Stornoway. We boarded the steamer at ten in the morning, sailing slowly down the Sound of Sleat and up to the Kyle of Lochalsh, where we waited for the afternoon tide. It was December and a bright, crisp day. Soon after we left, evening began to fall. I stood with my father on deck, silent and lost in thought. To the west the sun was sinking in a golden sky behind the dark shadows of the inner isles of Scalpay, Raasay and Rona, and the purple hills of Skye. To the east, a vast carpet of stars was being unrolled above the mountains of the mainland: Ben Bhan, Maol Chean-dhearg, and Ben Alligih, and great Ben Eighe towering above them all. We sailed between them into the night, out into the stormy waters of the North Minch. Hours passed in darkness, the steamer itself a tiny island ploughing through cold waters into the unknown. And then, out in the distance, a light appeared and was soon followed by others—the lights of Stornoway beckoning to us as if from beyond the world.

It was on those journeys with my father that the other side of my character was formed. He too had been brought up a Presbyterian, in a pious Calvinist family of Inverness, but he had early lost his faith. He thought of himself as a freethinker and a rationalist, and I suppose he was, though in some matters he was far from rational. Through him I learned to use my mind, to question all I was told in school or church. It took me much longer to learn to question what he said as well. By the time I was fifteen, I had joined him in my unfaith, a matter which my mother accepted with resignation. She was a Calvinist, after all, and to her everything was predestined. If I were one of the elect, it would not damn me to abandon my faith; if I were not, no amount of prayers or psalms or sermons would serve to bring me salvation.

I wonder now if I am saved or damned by what I have known. I fear damnation as not even the staunchest elder of my mother's church could fear it, and I doubt salvation as not even the most surely damned can doubt it. The words have held new meanings for me these three years and more.

* * *

LIKE MY FATHER, I continued my education at Aberdeen University. I studied sociology and politics. Mine was a purely academic interest: I never wanted to be a social worker or a politician. What drove me was curiosity, a strong urge to know how society worked, to uncover what lay beneath the surface appearance of human life.

By my fourth year, I had developed a particular interest in the sociology of religion. Whenever I thought about home, about the only society I knew at firsthand, I found myself coming back again and again to that unbreakable knot of religion that tied it all together. I read the classic texts—Durkheim, Weber, Tawney, and the rest—and moved on via Berger and Luckmann to Wilson and the study of sectarianism. And then I found that sects and churches were no longer the fashionable thing, that the attention of scholars had shifted to that great, amorphous mass of cults and philosophies brought together under the term New Religious Movements.

All this led quite naturally to my Ph.D., on which I spent another four years, this time in Glasgow. My subject was the social location of converts to the Unification Church (the Moonies) in Scotland. I stayed on in Glasgow for a couple of years as a junior lecturer on temporary contracts. My salary was a pittance, the workload heavy, the students unrewarding for the most part. But I stayed on, mainly because of Catriona.

We met in my second year in Glasgow, a

chance meeting at a party in a friend's flat, quick glances, a sense of recognition, mutual embarrassment, and a feeling in the pit of the stomach, a knowing: the irrational in its purest, dizziest sense. I remember the pang of disappointment when she left that night: we had barely exchanged ten words. I learned her name and that she had a Glaswegian accent, that was all. But her face and voice were fixed in my mind, for a time it seemed they *were* my mind, all it consisted of, all it would ever be. I knew then, that night, within minutes of seeing her, we both knew, that nothing would ever be the same again, that all had changed in a matter of moments. I had never fallen in love before, it was as though I had stepped, breathless, into a world I did not recognize.

My friend knew that her full name was Catriona Stuart and that she lived in Hamilton. He did not know her well, she was a friend of a friend, but he told me what he could: that she played or sang in a rock band, that she had a degree in psychology, that she had been a model for a famous artist, with whom she had lived for a time, and that she now lived with a boyfriend called Mark or Michael.

Almost none of these things turned out to be true. Catriona did, indeed, live in Hamilton, and she was a musician; but she did not play in a rock band, she was a violinist with a chamber music ensemble. She had posed several times for Kenneth Logan, a Glaswegian artist with a growing international reputation, and one of his paintings of her could be seen in the Burrell Collection. She took me to see it soon after we started going out together. I think it was her way of seducing me. We had not slept together then, and I was embarrassed by her nakedness, the vividness of her flesh. I was also astonished by the depth of Logan's perception, his understanding of Catriona, the obvious pleasure he had taken in her body.

She told me as we were leaving that she and Logan had never slept together. I sensed that that was not the whole truth, that they had had a complex relationship. But for the time being it satisfied me to know it. It was one less commitment in her past. As for the rest: her degree had been in philosophy and music, and her boyfriend Melvin had walked out on her almost a year before.

I learned all this later, this and much more. The second time we met was not by chance. Jamie, my friend, arranged it, though I did not know it then. At the time, it seemed like destiny to both of us; and perhaps that is what it was, perhaps Jamie was no more than a willing tool.

In the years since then I have often asked myself: what if I had gone somewhere else that night? What if Catriona had been ill? What if? . . . But there comes a point when all the what-ifs dry up and fall away. They really do not matter. We would still have met, the next day, the next week, the next year—that is the important thing, that we would have met somehow.

We went to the theater, Jamie, his girlfriend, Catriona, and myself. Everyone tried to pretend that it was just a casual arrangement: I was Jamie's friend, Catriona knew his girlfriend well, it was natural that we might end up meeting again. But we all knew the truth, and throughout the evening there was a faint air of embarrassment.

I walked Catriona home. It is among my sharpest memories, the shape of her head in the darkness, the motion of her body beside mine, the faint aroma of an unfamiliar perfume, an overpowering sense of expectancy. I remember nothing of what we talked about. All that happened happened in silence, at a level deeper than words. A movement, a glance, my hand brushing hers, her faint but unmistakable response. And later that night, much later, all movement ceasing.

WE LIVED TOGETHER for four years, Catriona and I, and we were married for two of them. I was happier than most men ever are, and I believe she was as well. Looking back, I know I was often careless with our time together, valued it for less than it was worth. I know better now, I treasure every moment in my memory.

There is no need for detail, our lives were perfectly ordinary. All you need to know can be summed up in a single sentence: Catriona died at the age of twenty-six, died of cancer, died at three in the morning while I was asleep.

THERE ARE MOMENTS, even now, when I torment myself with the question: was he working even then to bring me to him? And not just me, but Catriona too?

Chapter

2

THERE WAS NOTHING LEFT for me in Glasgow, no street that did not bear Catriona's mark, no landmark that did not remind me of her. I did my best with my grief. It never left me, but in time I came to live with it as with a wound or an amputated limb. Now, of course, it has been replaced by something else—something more like fear.

I returned home for several months. There are few places better than Lewis for being alone. It was summer, and most days I would drive to West Uig, to Mangurstadh Beach. In winter, that is one of the wildest places on earth. There is nothing beyond it but the open reaches of the north Atlantic. Seals come to the rocks, and further out the flukes of whales tilt above the water. All that summer, I sat alone on the beach, trying to empty my mind of thoughts I could not bear. If anyone had seen me, they might have thought me another rock thrown down on the sand.

On Sundays, I went with my mother to church, more for her comfort than my own. There was no God waiting for me there, and the pastor's promises of life eternal rang falsely in my ears. But it gave me a certain peace. I could almost pretend to be a child again, to have my life ahead of me, and Catriona.

My father saw a research post in sociology at Edinburgh University advertised in the *Times* Educational Supplement. I put it away at first, thinking it too early to return to my old life. But I could not go back to Glasgow, and I knew I could not face the long winter on Lewis. I applied for the job and was interviewed that August. In September, I arrived in Edinburgh with a small suitcase and a bag of books.

I remember that for a moment, as I stepped from the plane, I thought there was someone waiting for me, just out of sight. It was a fanciful notion. I knew no one in the city, and I had no desire for company.

Finding accommodation from a distance had proved difficult, and I spent my first two weeks in Edinburgh with a friend of the family, Dr. Ramsey McLean. He knew all about Catriona and the circumstances of her death, and I talked with him at some length about how hard I found it to cope with my loss. An Aberdonian, red faced and jovial, he had known my father at university and spent frequent summer vacations on Lewis. I had last seen him there two years earlier.

He helped me find my feet in the city, introducing me to friends in the university, where he worked in the health center, and providing me with bearings. Toward the end of the first fortnight, he told me that he had found an excellent flat for me. I moved in two days later.

The house in which he had found rooms stood toward the bottom end of the Royal Mile, in Bakehouse Close. Known as Deacon Laing's Land, it was a six-story tenement built in 1658 by a wealthy landowner turned Covenanter who, in the duke of Rothes's phrase, "glorified God in the Grassmarket" when he was hanged there for his beliefs. It had known vicissitudes, but when I came to live there showed no signs of the slum from which it had been transformed not long before. I had a small flat on the top floor, a series of oddly shaped, low-ceilinged rooms full of wainscoting and rambling plaster decoration, tastefully furnished.

IN THE MEANTIME, I had been settling in at work. My head of department was James Fergusson, the newly appointed professor of social anthropology. You may have read his work on urban renewal in the 1960s. He has served on more than one government commission and is believed to have ambitions, I could not tell you precisely of what sort.

We met the day after my arrival at his office in Buccleuch Place. He quickly made it clear to me that my appointment had been made against his wishes. Some of the theologians at New College had expressed a wish for some hard information about the city's reputedly numerous occult and magical groups.

There was a fear of satanism in the air, a mood of unease. Those of a fundamentalist persuasion within the churches argued that devil worship was alive and flourishing, that satanic abuse was on the increase. The more responsible thought this hyperbole, but found it hard either to deny reports of actual occult practices or to distinguish readily between simple New Age wooliness and more disturbing forays into demonism or black magic.

"Dr. Macleod," Fergusson began almost as soon as I had stepped through his door, "I have to tell you that I have the most severe reservations about your presence here. I run a department founded on rigor. You will find this an empirical establishment, not a haven for half-baked beliefs and mumbo jumbo."

I tried to reassure him. It was not easy, he was not an easy man to reach.

"I agree with you entirely," I said, "as far as the empirical approach is concerned. I'm not interested in these beliefs myself, I'm not a believer in any sense. But I do think it makes sense to study the irrational, to understand what social factors create groups like these. Don't you think that's worthwhile?"

"That's not what the men in black suits at New College are looking for. Or their chums in the Kirk. They want evidence of devil worship. Witchcraft. Demonic possession."

"I can't give them that, not if what they mean is evidence that any of those things is real. They already believe in a devil, in powers of darkness—they hardly need me to prove it to them. I intend to show them something different, that these occult activities involve nothing more than sad or inadequate people whose lives need a little drama."

"I've no time for psychology either."

"You won't get any. My investigations will be purely sociological. Hard facts about social class, education, actual and relative deprivation . . . "

Fergusson stood. He was a tall man, bearded, forbidding. I could see I had not reassured him.

"You miss the point, Dr. Macleod. I don't give a damn how hardheaded you are, how empirical your research will be. Your work here could give this department a bad name. Since I seem to have no choice in the matter, I'm forced to accommodate you. But I want some assurances. There are to be no public lectures on your findings. No lectures within the university without my express permission. No interviews with the press, local or national. In fact, no contact with members of the press. I want you to have a very low profile. Do you understand? I want to see as little of you round here as possible."

I agreed to his demands and turned to go.

"Dr. Macleod," he called out, catching me at the door. I looked back. "I understand you have had a personal tragedy."

I nodded.

"May I take it that this . . . loss will not interfere with your work?"

"I don't know what you mean."

"Of course you do. I want you to understand

that, if you can't handle this job, you'll have no sympathy from me. They have doctors at the health center to deal with personal problems. Our relationship is to remain strictly professional, purely academic." He paused. "And don't let me hear that you've been trawling the mediums in search of fond messages from your late beloved. I won't have that, I won't stand for it."

I wanted very much to hit him, but I did not. Instead I closed the door, quite hard, and went out, down the stairs, into the cold street. It had begun to rain, but I barely noticed it. I walked without a coat or a hat, not knowing where I was going or why. I was not angry with Professor Fergusson, what I felt was something beyond anger, much gentler, much more dangerous. In the end I came to myself and found a bus to take me back to town. I counted the stairs to my flat: there were one hundred and sixty-eight. Hard stone steps worn away in places by generations of feet, from landing to weary landing.

I spent the next few days tidying my books and papers or going for walks in order to explore the city—the Old Town first, then the straighter streets of the New Town with its elegant Georgian doorways and wrought-iron railings. I felt separate from everything, remote, dislocated, more like a tourist than a new resident. Nothing beautiful moved me, there was nothing harmonious in the long vistas or the tall sandstone facades.

I started work the following week, reading from early morning on into the evening at the National Library on George IV Bridge. So began a tedious drift into winter, each day marked out by a succession of books and pamphlets of mind-numbing banality. I wanted to familiarize myself with a broad range of New Age and occult beliefs, in order to narrow down my field of enquiry. I read until my eyes ached about the Great Pyramid, UFOs, ley lines, reincarnation, astrology, ancient mysteries of every kind, the Gnostic Gospels, enneagrams, tarot, Tantric yoga, crystal healing—a maze of theories that seemed to cover every imaginable human obsession, every hope and fear.

I skimmed the surface of it all like a skater who fears thin ice and a plunge into deep, ice-cold waters. Most of the books I read were trite, poorly executed, badly written, and repetitive. I had to remind myself daily that I was not there to sit in judgment, but to understand.

By the end of December I persuaded myself that I had read as much as I needed. I knew my way, stumblingly but accurately enough, across this unfamiliar terrain: sufficient to hold my own in conversations, to formulate my first, faltering questions, to grasp, with some effort, the answers I might be given. I made my first contact with some of the city's esoteric groups, restricting myself to the more popular and mainstream among them.

I reasoned—and was in due course proved correct—that direct contact with magical or satanic groups might be difficult to establish. These were people who either had something to hide or fancied they did—they would not rush out of the shadows to be interviewed by the first passerby. But I had read enough about the occult underworld to know that groups shaded into one another, as did beliefs and practices. Those who practiced magic or demonism today had in all likelihood started out attending meetings of much milder associations, with Subud or Theosophy or Rosicrucianism, or one of the circles devoted to the teachings of Ouspensky or Gurdjieff.

A sociologist is not a journalist and cannot afford to work like one. Where the journalist can write a prize-winning article on the basis of a single visit or half a dozen interviews and is free to offend or misrepresent since he need never return again, the sociologist needs to tread warily. He may have to spend months gradually coming to know the people whose behavior and beliefs he is researching, winning their confidence, discarding first impressions, inspiring revelations of their deeper feelings and convictions. It is delicate work, calling for human understanding as much as scientific detachment.

So it was that most evenings found me in damp, ill-heated rooms or rented halls, listening to talks on Atlantis, the Himalayan masters, hermetic lore, or alchemy. The speakers were surprisingly varied. Many belonged to an earlier generation, itself the heir of late Victorian occultism. Intense, shabby, or a little overdressed, their speech full of archaisms, they presided over gatherings of the long-term faithful. Dust filled the rooms in which they spoke, old rooms lined with shelves of arcane books with unreadable titles. I would pass into a half sleep as their voices droned on about astral bodies or the lost continent of Lemura.

Others were much younger, a new generation

of enthusiasts, more interested in morphic reso-
nance or corn circles than the tired fantasies of
Madame Blavatsky and Annie Besant. It was
among them, I thought, that I would make my first
contacts with the people I most wanted to meet. I
listened carefully, biding my time, gaining their
trust, waiting to see who talked most of the magical
arts, who hinted at things they might say if they
chose to but which they thought it best to conceal. I
told no one I was a university researcher, knowing
the suspicion it might provoke; instead, I let people
believe I was a mature student in the Sociology
department. Later, when some of them knew me
better and trusted me, I might reveal the truth.

During the days, I continued my studies in the
library. By February, my life was divided between it
and the rooms where I attended my almost nightly
lectures. I visited the university very seldom, to pick
up mail and remind Fergusson that I was still alive.
My reading habits changed. I had covered enough
of the general literature to get by in discussions and
the chitchat that inevitably followed the meetings I
attended, but I was still largely ignorant of the
world I hoped to penetrate.

I found all the books I could on magic, beginning with Eliphas Lévi's *Dogme et rituel de la haute
magie* and sundry works of Aleister Crowley, before
going on to Ficino and Dee. Dark mysteries, arcane
secrets, and page after page of gibberish. I found it
wearying work, ploughing through it all, not in
search of truth or power, but as a means to fashion-
ing a mask for myself.

But a mask is only a mask, and if it is tied on

with string, so much the more visible. I needed something more than the names of authors I had read and jargon I had mastered. In the middle of April, I started to practice some of the rites prescribed in the books of ritual magic I had read so far. I chalked circles and pentagrams on my bare floorboards, lit candles, recited incantations in Latin, Greek, Old French, Middle English, and languages I did not even recognize.

At first I felt ridiculous, but as time passed and I grew familiar with the rituals, I began to find them curiously relaxing, almost hypnotic. That in itself was interesting, and I determined to consult someone in the psychology department. It might be possible to explain involvement in occultism by a need for ritual and the psychological comforts it could bring. I understood nothing then, I was still a child.

Chapter 3

SPRING PASSED, AND SUMMER. The musty, book-lined rooms grew a little warmer, the dust thickened on the shelves and was visible in sudden, unexpected shafts of sunlight that seemed to come from a different world. I had no time for anything but work, I wanted nothing but to wrap myself in it as a shield against the pain that dogged me, ready at any moment to hurl itself on my back and pull me to the ground.

I did, however, make a couple of friends. In late August, I started to lead a series of seminars for staff and postgraduate students at New College, the Church of Scotland Seminary on the Mound. They were organized by a lecturer of roughly my own age called Iain Gillespie. Although he was an ordained minister, he preferred academic work to running a parish, and I quickly found him to be open-minded and genuinely interested in my research.

He came with me to some meetings of the Theosophists and Rosicrucians, and I lent him some of my books. A few of his more fundamentalist colleagues had warned him of what they considered the growing peril of satanic child abuse, and he was keen to find out what he could for himself.

"I don't believe most of those stories," I told him after a seminar in which the subject had been raised. "I've seen no real evidence that what is involved is more than childish imagination. Your evangelical friends need satanic abuse in order to confirm their belief that the devil is at work in the world today. Since I don't believe in a devil, I find it hard to credit the stories they put about."

"You're probably right," he said. "I don't believe in a devil either, at least, not one with horns and a tail. But I do believe in evil. There are evil men, evil actions, even evil places. I think you should take care where you go and who you talk to."

"I'll be all right," I assured him. "These people are sad, not evil."

He brought me home for dinner several times, and introduced me to his wife, Harriet. They lived in Dean Village, in a modern flat overlooking the Water of Leith. As I had expected, they were both regular churchgoers, but I found them disinclined to preach or question. I made my own agnosticism clear to Harriet early on, and that was almost the last that was ever said on the subject.

Harriet taught English at the Mary Erskine School, one of the city's three Merchant Company academies, a short drive from Dean Village, at the other end of Ravelston Dykes. We discovered a mutual love of Hardy and a common distaste for much modern literature. She knew no Gaelic, and I found myself promising one evening after we had eaten that I would teach her a little, so she might read some of the fine poetry my father had read to me from childhood.

In September, I started to spend an increasing amount of time with one group in particular, the Fraternity of the Old Path. They owned a house in Ainslie Place, a delightful oval of Georgian dwellings in the New Town, donated around the turn of the century by a leading devotee. Small in numbers though they were, they proved in many ways the most interesting of the many groups I studied. They held a set of doctrines centered round the belief that true knowledge had been lost after the fall of Rome and that gnosis could only be obtained today through the performance of elaborate rituals loosely based on what was known of the ancient Greek and Egyptian mysteries. By performing the rites in the correct frame of mind and with due attentiveness, the acolyte might hope to reach a state of divine ecstasy in which gnosis would be poured into him like wine into an empty vessel. They needed neither drugs nor sex to attain union with their higher selves—or so they claimed.

They permitted me to attend many of their ceremonies, ceremonies which, in all honesty, I found to be no more than ragged pantomimes based on a limited familiarity with the rites they sought to imitate. Greek and Latin words and phrases were mixed indiscriminately and with little accuracy; early Egyptian divinities were invoked alongside foreign importations of the Ptolemaic period; costumes fashioned from pictures in popular books of Egyptology made the rites seem not unlike scenes from an amateur operatic society's production of *Aïda*; and broad Scottish accents called incongruously on dead gods of the desert and the starry wastes of Thebes

Yet there was a terrible seriousness in their voices and an assumed dignity in their long-rehearsed movements that transcended all the tawdriness and inarticulate striving after grace. Like their originals in the dim candlelit temples of Isis or Mithras, they somehow achieved an elevation, a discarding of the everyday self and the putting on of new robes in a new consciousness. At times the discordant jangling of cymbals and the taut repetition of muffled drums gave way to a muted harmony that embraced all present. And I sensed that, for some of them at least, the mysteries of Horus might be no more than a vestibule leading to a vast hall occupied by older and darker gods.

There was another attraction for me in the Fraternity of the Old Path: their extensive library of books on the occult. By the late spring, I found the resources of the National Library yielding less and less to whet my growing appetite for esoteric reading matter. Indeed, I had begun to suspect that the library staff were reluctant or for some reason unable to provide me with many of the volumes I needed. In particular, certain older texts, works on magic dating from the fifteenth and sixteenth centuries, were declared unavailable or subject to severe restrictions. I would be told that a binding was loose or the paper fragile or the volume missing, presumed stolen.

I began to frequent secondhand and antiquarian bookshops in the hope of tracking down a few items I needed to consult on a regular basis, works like Walker's *Spiritual and Demonic Magic from Ficino to Campanella* and Waite's *Real History of the Rosicrucians*. From time to time I would stumble across something of interest, but the occult sections of these shops were dispiriting jumbles, their shelves crammed for the most part full of naive popularizations and sensational books on the "mysteries of the universe." Once, I found a copy of Scott's translation of Ficino's Latin translation of the *Corpus Hermeticum*. But I could never track down anything published earlier than the nineteenth century, though I looked hard enough. I never even bothered to travel to shops in London, where such treasures might well be come by, for I knew without asking that they would be well outside my price range.

When I explained the situation to the Fraternity's librarian, a white-haired Pole called Jurczyk, he agreed at once to let me have free access to any books that might be of use to me, provided I read them on the premises. I guessed that he was only too delighted to have a serious enquirer making use of his precious but virtually unread collection. He gave me a key and detailed instructions about lights, heating, and locking up. I began to spend my days at Ainslie Place. Sometimes I would read from morning until late at night. No one ever disturbed me there, it was a dim, quiet room in an empty house. I had as much solitude as I wanted. There were days on end when I spoke with no one. I would go from my rooms in Canongate directly to Ainslie Place and shut myself up there in that little library. There was sunlight through the streets all summer, but I saw little of it. The darkness had begun to fold itself about me. I had my books; they were all I wanted.

As autumn came on and the days shortened, I grew a little uneasy in the library at night. It was often dark when I left, the streets not quite deserted, but hushed. The sound of my footsteps would carry long distances in the silence. I would hurry home to my little fire and go to bed uneasy. At the start of October I started to have bad dreams. They would waken me in the middle of the night, but I could never remember what it was that had frightened me. All that remained when I woke was the sound of a sibilant voice whispering in my ears, as though someone had been bending down beside my pillow. Someone I should not like to have set eyes upon.

It was late in November that matters began to take a more sinister turn. I arrived at the Fraternity's headquarters later than usual, about nine o'clock at night. It was a Friday, and I knew no one would be about. I had been occupied all day with a group of Iain's students, to whom I had been invited to explain the nature and direction of my researches.

A meal had followed, together with some close questioning from Iain's head of department, the Reverend Professor Craigie. He wanted to see me again the following day in order to pursue several important questions I had been unable to answer to his satisfaction, and I had no choice but to dig more deeply into some volumes I knew I might find in the Fraternity library.

The Fraternity's rooms occupied two floors of a three-story building. The ground floor was occupied by a large and a small meeting room, a small kitchen, a bathroom, and a storage room where the regalia and other ritual equipment were kept. Upstairs were the office, the guest room, where visitors were allowed to stay for one or two nights, and the library, which had been created from three smaller rooms.

The third floor was empty. It had previously been rented from the Fraternity by the Misses Frazer, spinster members of the group almost since its inception. They had, so Mr. Jurczyk told me, died at a greatly advanced age a year or so earlier, within three days of one another. The Fraternity had not yet got round to finding new tenants.

That night, climbing the stairs in that dark building, I felt myself more than usually apprehensive of the silent rooms all round me. For the first time in months, I had spent an extended period with people like myself, students and academics, young people who did not spend their spare time dressing up in operatic costumes or discussing the esoteric intricacies of the Kabbalah and Sanskrit lore. Returning to these cold, gloomy rooms was like reentering an underground cave after a spell in the sunshine.

As I reached the first landing, I half turned, as if I had heard or sensed something in the shadows behind me. But there was nothing there. I glanced up the staircase that led upward into the empty flat above. All seemed still. I walked on to the library and went inside.

There was no central light, only green-shaded desk lamps at the four tables and individual lights above each stack of shelves. I switched on the light of the stack nearest me and made my way to the nearest desk.

I cannot be sure—it is a memory so overlaid by later impressions—but I believe that, as I stretched out my hand to put on the desk lamp, I heard a sound. It was as though someone on the other side of the table had drawn a deep, sighing breath. The next moment, the lamp was lit and I could see no one. I shook myself and all but said out loud, "Pull yourself together; there's nothing to be afraid of."

I sat down and opened my briefcase, arranging my notebooks and papers on the desk as usual. Gradually, the familiarity of what I was doing began to take effect, calming me, returning me to a sense of safe, undramatic routine. I stood and went to a stack on my right, where I guessed that several of the volumes I needed would be located. They were all there, and I quickly became engrossed in the pursuit of the answers I sought.

Back at the table, I buried myself in my work, leafing through book after book, scribbling notes, consulting my index cards. From time to time I would get up and go across to a stack for a book I needed, sometimes I would consult the catalogue. The pile of books on my desk grew quite high.

The work went better than I had hoped, and I became wholly absorbed in it, shutting out all impressions beyond the pale circle of light that the lamp cast over the tabletop and my papers. It must have been midnight or later when I went back to the shelves for the last time.

As I bent to pick up a book from the bottom shelf of a stack I had not been to before, I noticed the edge of a small volume jutting out from behind the wooden back of the bookcase, at a spot where the carpenter had left a space. With difficulty, I succeeded in catching a firm enough grip on it to draw it out through the gap. It seemed old, older than the majority of volumes I had seen there before. Curious, I took it over to my table and sat down.

The little book was bound in hard brown leather. It had no title on the spine or the front cover. In size it was little more than five by four inches, and I guessed it held around two hundred pages. The binding suggested a date at least before 1700, possibly much older. Taking care not to bend the spine unduly—the general state of the volume suggested that it had not been opened for a very long time—I gently lifted the cover. Unlike all the other books I had seen in the library, this had no label to identify it as the property of the Fraternity.

The flyleaf bore a faded inscription in brownish ink, written in an archaic and, to me, illegible hand. I turned it and came straightaway to the title page. This read as follows:

Avimetus Africanus,
Kalibool Kolood
aw
Resaalatool Shams ilaal Helaal
sive
Matrix Aeternitatis
aut
Epistola solis ad lunam crescentem
cum versione Latina et notis D. Konigii
And newly Englished by
Nicholas Ockley
Paris, apud Christophorum Beys, Plantini Nepotem
MDXCVIII

It astonished me to find a book printed as early as 1598 lying here gathering dust behind some shelves, unopened and unread. I had never come across the title in my reading, but that was hardly surprising. All the same, I knew at once that it was an early example of printed occult literature, possibly a treatise on astrology. This first impression was confirmed as soon as I opened the book and began to leaf through it.

The left-hand pages carried text that I guessed to be Arabic, printed in large letters. Facing these were pages set in double columns, one in Latin, the other in English. The main text consisted of short verses, which I then took to be spells, interspersed with what appeared to be commentary or instructions. Of these, one in particular struck me at the time. I still have it by heart.

Hee that shal come shal come quickly
And hee shal bring with him many

For that there are now with him many
And hee with them always untill hee come.
Call on him thus and bee not afraide:
Ya maloon, ya shaytoon, ya rabb al-mawt
Bismika, bismika, ya rabb al-mawt.

Every five pages or so a reproduction of a talis-manic device—a circle or a star filled with geomet-rical shapes and more Arabic writing—was printed opposite a page of instructions on its use.

I continued reading, fascinated by the curiosity of the language and the strange, oracular quality of the spells. The author, I learned from Ockley's fore-word, had been a Moroccan scholar, known to medieval Europe by the Latin name Avimetus (or Avimetus Africanus). His treatise was a little-known classic of ritual magic that had exercised a profound influence on authors such as Trithemius and Cornelius Agrippa and had been condemned by Johann Wier for its "diabolic incantations" and its advocacy of "consort with all manner of demons."

Tired from my hours of note taking, my mind turned readily enough to the relatively unde-manding task of poring over a book not directly connected with my paper. I read on, lulled by the lateness of the hour, the silence, the dim lighting, and my own fatigue, entranced by the weird lilting verses and their haunting tone. I understood very little.

As I turned a page toward the end, I saw, not a pentagram or a talisman as I had expected, but a woodcut illustration. It took me about half a minute to disentangle the subject and composition of the drawing, but to this day I wish I had never done so. I closed the book with a shudder and thrust it from me; but printed on my mind's eye were shapes and figures of unspeakable horror. It had been no more than a glimpse, but in that moment of recognition I had seen forms that I will never forget as long as I live.

The woodcut depicted not an Eastern scene as might have been expected, but one set in Europe, the interior of a large church, huge and vaulted, with shadows on both sides of a wide nave. Thick carved pillars divided the nave from the side aisles, and a heavy curtain hung in front of the chancel, blocking all the eastern end of the church from view.

Along one side were ranged several stone tombs topped with monuments. One near the chancel end had been opened, a great iron door swung back. On the ground lay what I took to be corpses, as though they had been dragged from their resting places and scattered in the aisle. That was sufficiently revolting in itself to make me shudder, but it was not the real horror of the drawing.

Just visible in the opening of the tomb were several indistinct figures, stooped over the remains of the dead. They had short, stumpy bodies, naked bodies the colour of parchment, white meat, bloodless, eternally pale. They were bent over the corpses, sucking and nibbling. And one . . . Dear God, I cannot forget this—one was turning its head to look directly at the viewer. It did not have a face exactly, and it was shrouded in a piece of rotting cloth, but I could tell that it had no eyes. It had no eyes, but I knew that it could see.

I slammed the book shut and sat back, stupefied by the obscenity of the woodcut I had happened on. One thing I knew with absolute certainty, and I know it now without any hint of doubt—whoever the artist was who had penned that loathsome scene had not imagined it, but had drawn it from life.

As I sat there, glancing nervously about me, I became aware for the first time that there were noises in the room above me. Something told me that they had been there for some time, but engrossed as I had been in my reading, I had failed to notice them. I strove to make out what they could be. A sort of flapping and scraping that moved slowly across the floor above my head. At first I thought it must be a member of the Fraternity who had come to investigate the lights, or that, perhaps, the apartment upstairs had been rented without my knowledge.

But even as I listened, something in the quality of the sounds told me that, whatever was making them, it was not human. My heart seemed to freeze as the noises moved across the room in the direction of the door that led to the first-floor landing. I heard the door opening, and the sound moving across a wooden floor. Terrified, I went to the door of the library. Somewhere above me, I could hear it, very soft, like seaweed on damp rocks, flapping and wriggling across the landing.

As I stood listening, it reached the first step and started down the stairs.

Chapter

4

I CAN SCARCELY REMEMBER how I got out of the building. I gathered my books and papers together in any order, rammed them into my briefcase, and made for the door, leaving library books scattered across my desk and lights burning. I did not pause to listen to the sounds that were audible from the staircase now, but dashed down to the ground floor and through the front door, all but falling down the steps onto the pavement.

I did not halt for breath or thought until I was back in my rooms in Canongate. The journey back, made on foot, was a constant terror. I half walked, half ran through the streets of the New Town, through Charlotte Square to the West End, then along the more dimly lit stretches of the Old Town, below the Castle, then up into Lawnmarket and so back at last to Canongate and Bakehouse Close. Each time I passed the unlit entrance to a close or court, I would hurry past, as though fearful that something lurked there unseen.

By the time I reached my rooms I was exhausted. I turned on all the lights and sat for half an hour, shaking, slowly collecting myself. I put a record on my stereo and played it softly, Bach violin concertos, the most soothing music I could find; gradually, the music and the familiar surroundings began to restore me to a sense of normality. Two cups of coffee revived my nerves and mind, and I was soon able to take stock of what had happened. It seemed obvious enough. I had overworked myself recently, buried myself in matters likely to lend themselves to morbid brooding, spent too little time in normal company, going to concerts, visiting the theater. The lateness of the hour and the eeriness of my surroundings had combined to produce in my overwrought and exhausted brain an abnormal reaction to a perfectly ordinary sixteenth-century woodcut. That reaction had itself brought on an aural hallucination, and I had panicked and fled. So I reasoned at the time.

It was about three in the morning when I finally went to bed, tired out both physically and mentally. I fell asleep at once. I remember nothing of my dreams, nor do I know precisely what it was that woke me. All I recall is that I started out of sleep with an indefinable yet powerful sense of dread, a feeling that the darkened room around me was alive with something even darker. It must have been about four-thirty, with dawn still some time away. Gradually, the first feelings of panic started to subside, but, even as they did so, I became conscious of sounds above the ceiling of my room.

These were not the flapping and scraping noises I had heard above the library, but seemed more like footsteps. At first I thought it must be someone in the room above me pacing his floor, unable to sleep. Then I remembered that there was no room above mine.

When the building had been reconstructed in the early eighties, on account of the curious shape of the roof, the sixth floor—the one just above mine—was too small to allow for a full-size apartment. Instead, there were a couple of single rooms let out to students and a long section where the roof came within three feet or less of the floor. I knew that this section stretched across my apartment. I also knew that it had been bricked up and closed for good. There was no way in or out of it.

I lay in bed in the dark, sweating as I listened to the backward and forward movement of the sounds above me. I could make them out more clearly now and, with a feeling of the most intense horror, I realized that they could not have been made by human feet. They possessed a quality that reminded me somehow of the creatures I had seen in the woodcut, sucking the corpses on the church floor. The image of that scene came back to me then with renewed vividness, and nothing I could do would expunge from my mind the sight of that eyeless thing, half turned, with its mouth set at an abnormal angle.

I do not know how long I lay there listening, paralyzed, unable to reach out for the light or otherwise break the horrified trance into which I had fallen. Dawn came at last, pale and weak at first, the light gradually strengthening as it filtered through my curtains. As the darkness was gradually dispelled, the sounds seemed to grow weaker until they finally faded completely. I fell into a deep and dreamless sleep.

I SLEPT THROUGH ALL of the next day, a Saturday, and neither dreams nor sounds disturbed me. I did not wake, not that day, not that night. Yet one faint memory has remained at the back of my mind. Whenever I clutch at it and try to drag it into the full light of consciousness, it evaporates and is gone. But at unguarded moments it returns.

It was already in my mind when I finally woke on Sunday morning: the image of a dark stone doorway, hugely arched and gaping. Beyond it glistening stone steps led down into the deepest blackness imaginable. That is all. Sometimes I think that I must have stood staring at that vast doorway through all the hours I slept, never moving, never blinking, as though waiting for someone—or something—to emerge. Or was I expected to set foot on those steps, to pass through the doorway and descend into the blackness below?

I was woken shortly after nine on Sunday by the sound of knocking at my door. As I struggled to regain consciousness, I realized that I had lost all track of the day or the time. The knocking came again, and I called out feebly. A voice answered from behind the door.

"Andrew, are you there? Are you all right?"

It was Iain. I had asked him to call on Sunday morning in order to go over my proposals for the next seminar.

With an enormous effort, as if tearing myself from cords tying me to the bed, I pulled myself up. My head ached intolerably, and I felt nauseated. Throwing aside my bedclothes, I struggled to stand and managed to make my way to the door. As it opened, I saw Iain's concerned face, then, unable to stand any longer, I collapsed onto the floor.

I came round later to find Iain hovering anxiously over me. He had dragged me back to the bed and made me as comfortable as possible. I tried to sit up, but he pushed me back firmly, saying I should take it easy until the doctor arrived. He had rung the university health service, and they had said someone would be along soon.

Twenty minutes later I saw Dr. McLean come through the door. By good fortune, he had been on duty that morning. I was relieved to see him rather than some indifferent locum who did not know me from Adam.

He examined me briskly but carefully, and at last pronounced himself satisfied. Packing away his stethoscope and blood-pressure meter, he snapped shut his little case and turned to me.

"Well, Andrew, I have to say I'm very disappointed in you. I'd taken you for a man with greater sense. Do your parents know what sort of state you've got yourself into?"

"My parents? I haven't . . . " I realized that it had been some time now since I had spoken to either of them.

"No matter. It's none of my business if you speak to them or not. But I wish you would. I think you need to talk to someone."

"What's wrong with me?" I felt wretched, and the tone of his voice suggested something serious.

"Oh, nothing much," he said. "Nothing I haven't seen more often than I like. You're overworked. Your nervous system's been taxed to its limit. And you haven't got over the death of your young woman. I'll call it nervous fatigue and leave it at that."

"Is that all?" I was relieved. The way I felt, I was sure there was something more serious the matter.

"All?" His heavy eyebrows knotted and he looked down at me severely. "You'll wreck your health permanently if you don't do something about it. I could give you tranquilizers, but they'll do nothing but mask the symptoms and let you think you can get away with overdoing things. Instead, I'm going to prescribe an herbal tonic and plenty of rest. I want you to stay in bed for the next week. After that, you can take some mild exercise, go for the odd walk, but take it easy. There's to be absolutely no writing or serious reading, and no intellectual conversation of any description. You can watch television if you like, provided you stick to light programs.

"If you allow yourself to relax and take it easy for a few weeks, I guarantee you'll be right as rain in no time. Once you're back on your feet, there's no reason you shouldn't carry on with your work, provided you get out more and find some distractions."

He chatted for a while longer. I asked him to contact my parents, and he said he would. Finally, he looked at his watch and said he had another patient waiting. As he reached the door, however, he turned and looked at me.

"There's just one wee thing, Andrew," he said. "Would you mind telling me how you got those marks on your face and hands?"

"Marks?" I looked at my hands in puzzlement. To my astonishment, I found several angry red weals, circular in shape, each about the size of a one-penny coin.

I shook my head and said that this was the first time I had ever noticed them. He looked strangely at me.

"Well, they're very mysterious," he said. "When I first saw them, I thought they might be a rash of some sort. Then I took a closer look and saw they were all contusions, as if the skin had been pressed or sucked very hard, leaving some bruising. They should heal quickly enough. But surely you have some idea of how you came by them?"

"No," I said, in all honesty. I could not imagine anything that could have caused such marks, unless I had injured myself while asleep.

"Well," said Dr. McLean, "I'll keep an eye on them. I'll call in tomorrow. And if I catch you reading, you'll be in serious trouble."

He left, and I leaned back against the pillows. I was tired, in spite of having slept for so long. My sleep had been unrefreshing, but I felt afraid to shut my eyes. I avoided looking at my hands, and I knew that, if I went to the bathroom, I would not look in the mirror. For all I could think of, when I remembered the marks that had so puzzled Dr. McLean, was a group of white-fleshed creatures sucking the bodies of the dead in an old woodcut.

Chapter 5

DR. McLEAN RANG MY PARENTS later that same morning, and on Monday my mother flew in from Stornoway. I was, I must confess, profoundly glad to have her there. She did not reproach me for having been in touch so little, made no attempt to preach to me about my overworking, and fussed as little as possible under the circumstances. I was grateful for her down-to-earthness, for knowing that the matters which had preoccupied my waking thoughts for so long would have meant less than nothing to her.

Dr. McLean visited regularly. His herbal tonic was slow to act, but by the second week I had begun to feel its benefit. By then I had moved from the bedroom to the living room, where I sat in an armchair and did jigsaws or played endless games of backgammon with my mother, who thought it rather sinful but indulged me so long as we did not gamble. When I read, I restricted myself to detective novels and Thomas Hardy. Nothing morbid or speculative was allowed to unsettle me.

Iain and Harriet visited me almost every day. Harriet brought me books, and I gave her some simple Gaelic lessons, much to my mother's amusement. I did not talk of my experiences, nor did anyone ask. The marks on my hands and face healed rapidly and were gone by the end of the second week.

By then I had started to take short walks in my mother's company. She had never been to Edinburgh before, and I was able to show her the sights, though it was soon apparent that I knew them almost as little as she. We were at first restrained in one another's company. We had never been close, never talked about things that might have mattered. Our conversations as we walked were brittle, formal exchanges. If our talk led us into dangerous territory, we would both draw back, as though by mutual agreement, and comment on the buildings or the view.

Several times we took a bus to Inverleith, to walk in the Botanical Gardens. She had never seen tropical plants before, or cacti, or palm trees as high as a tall house. As we walked through the glass houses, breathing hot, humid air utterly unlike the air of Lewis, she grew more relaxed. And one day, sitting beside a lily pond, she told me about a man she had loved before my father, who had died in a boating accident off Sula Sgeir. She had never talked about him to my father or to anyone else before. We sat together in a green light, each with a separate grief, sharing a secret for the first time in our lives.

"Come back home for Christmas, Andrew," she said. "You'll only fret here on your own. We missed you last year. It's not the same, just the two of us."

I had not even thought of Christmas. A few weeks earlier, I would have turned down the suggestion flat. It was not that I disliked Stornoway or that I was not fond of my parents. it was just that I did not think they were what I needed then. But what did I need? Not myself, certainly, not my loneliness, not Christmas in a city without friends. I said I would go back with her.

We left the following week. Dr. McLean had declared me fit to travel and thought Christmas at home would be the best medicine I could have. My father was waiting at the airport, and that evening there were old friends for dinner. I had not thought I would welcome company, but by the time the evening ended I had recaptured parts of myself I had thought lost for good.

The weather stayed fine over all the holiday and into the New Year. It was bitterly cold, but every day we woke to clear skies and a calm sea. On Christmas Day I went to church with my mother. My father stayed behind as he always did, though it would have comforted me that year if he had been there. God was not there, hidden in some corner of our little kirk or mysteriously present in the psalms; but the sound of my mother's voice and the childhood familiarity of those plain surroundings were enough to chase away the shadows that had been gathering round me in the past few months.

I flew back after New Year, ready to return to work in a more positive spirit. My father had exacted a promise from me that I would not brood on the past and that I would keep away from the morbid themes of my earlier research. I came back to my rooms in Canongate brimming with good resolutions, my head clear, and my nerves at rest. I slept well that night, and all my dreams were of Catriona. In the morning I woke rested and ready to get back to work. There was winter sunshine in my bedroom, and the only sounds I could hear came from the early traffic on the Royal Mile.

I spent the morning catching up on things at the department. James Fergusson was as unpleasant as ever; but he had heard of my illness and said he hoped I had made a good recovery. He even admitted that he had had good reports from New College on my research. I thanked him and escaped, vowing to keep out of his way until the end of term at least.

I had lunch with Iain in a pub in the High Street.

"I'm glad to see you on your feet again," he said. "I was worried that first day. You looked dreadful."

"I didn't feel too good. But I am a lot better. There's nothing like a spell on the islands to set a man on his feet again."

He shivered.

"Not for me," he said. "I'm a city man. The thought of a winter on Lewis puts the fear of God in me. All those storms, and nowhere to go. I like people around me, some sort of life. It would drive me mad up there. Nothing but storms and nowhere to go."

I sipped my whisky and shook my head.

"I'd sooner risk the islands than here. Edinburgh hasn't exactly lifted my spirits."

"You haven't given it a chance."

"No doubt. But you've not been fair on the islands either. Have you never been there?"

He shook his head.

"Well, then," I said, "if I try to love Edinburgh, maybe you'll come with me to Stornoway for a week or two in the summer."

We drank to our agreement, and then talked about how best to go on with my seminars. I told Iain I needed a couple of weeks to get back into the swing of things and to catch up on my notes. I still had not found the answers to all the questions Craigie had put to me before my illness.

"Take all the time you like," he said. "None of us is going anywhere."

"Two weeks," I said. "Give me two weeks to get everything in order."

"Fair enough. I'll fix it up for the seventeenth, that should give you enough time."

ON RETURNING TO MY ROOMS, I decided it was time to pick up my work where I had left off. My books and papers had been put away by Iain, and I had not so much as looked at them since the night of the disturbance in Ainslie Place.

The papers I had been working on then had been stuffed into my briefcase, and it in turn had been shoved to the back of a wardrobe in my bedroom. I brought it to the little room I used as a study and set it on my desk. From it I took the books and papers I had rammed inside in my panic over a month earlier. The papers were crumpled and torn, and I set to work flattening and straightening them.

As I reached the end, I glanced inside the briefcase and saw a sheet of crumpled paper. Lifting it out, I noticed a book underneath. It seemed disturbingly familiar. I reached into the case and lifted it out. It was bound in black leather, very dusty, obviously old—the very same volume that had woken that flapping, creeping thing in the darkness and left an image in my brain that nothing could wipe out.

I DO NOT KNOW HOW LONG I sat there, staring at the title page of that horrid little book, unable to move, unable to order my thoughts. The book itself I would not open farther, for fear of what I might see in it. My rational mind, so newly hardened by my stay at home and the conversations I had had with my father, insisted that no harm could come from something so trivial. Yet the thought of seeing again those pages of incantations, of catching sight of that grotesque woodcut, filled me with the deepest loathing.

Finally I stood, picked the book from the desk, and hurled it into my open briefcase. I knew there could be no other course of action for me but to return the book to the library from which it had come. Thinking of the carelessness that had allowed it to slip to the back of a bookcase and lie forgotten there for who could say how long, I imagined that no one would yet have noticed its disappearance. Nevertheless, it seemed important to me that no one should suspect me of theft. And I wanted to be rid of the thing, wanted it locked up where no one might find it again.

The thought of returning to that room alone was most uncomfortable. I knew that Jurczyk spent three afternoons a week there—Mondays, Wednesdays, and Fridays, from one to four. Today was a Wednesday, but to make doubly sure of having company, I telephoned. Jurczyk answered and expressed surprise at not having seen me for some weeks.

"I've been ill," I said. "But I've just come across something belonging to you. Would you mind if I came over now?"

"I'll be gone in an hour," he said.

"It won't take long. And I really would like to get this off my hands."

"I'll wait for you."

THE STREET WAS AS SILENT AS EVER, the old house as gray. Nothing had changed. I climbed the steps to the front door and rang the bell. The ringing echoed in the empty hallway, recalling unpleasant memories. My heart was beating too quickly. I felt an urge to turn and run away. With difficulty, I fought it down and remained where I was.

Jurczyk took his time in coming. He was slow on his legs, half-crippled by arthritis. But at last I heard the sound of his feet in the passage, shuffling toward the door. When he saw me, his wrinkled face broke into a smile.

"Mr. Macleod! It's very good to see you again. You say you have been ill. We are all so worried."

"I'm much better now. I'd just been . . . over-working. Nothing serious."

"Well, I am most glad to hear it. Come in, you must not to stand in the cold."

I passed through the door, gently closing it behind me. As I did so, I glanced apprehensively at the stairs and the dimly lit landing above; nothing moved in the untouched stillness. But I had to struggle to control the unease I felt at returning to this place.

Jurczyk led the way up the stairs and down the short passage to the library. He crept along slowly, and I walked beside him, shortening my stride and slowing my pace to accommodate his hesitant, shambling steps. I had time to examine the dark prints that hung on the walls, dust covered and redolent of a much earlier time. The house seemed to have stood still, to have remained unaltered over decades, as though reluctant to part with long-kept secrets. We walked without sound across a heavy carpet, dull red in color and seemingly as old as the house; my ears strained for sounds from the floor above or from the wainscoting all round me, but nothing stirred. Jurczyk opened the library door and we went in.

He sat down at his little desk and I drew up a

chair beside him. There was no one else there. The
lights were low. What little illumination came from
outside was already fading. I began to apologize for
having left so abruptly on my last visit here, leaving
lights lit and books scattered about the desk I had
been using. He looked at me strangely from behind
thick glasses, a look of puzzlement on his narrow
face. A lock of white hair tumbled onto his forehead, and he raised a hand to push it back in place.

"I am sorry," he said, "but I do not understand.
You are surely mistaken. I was here on the Monday
afternoon after you are here. No lights were lit. All
the books were in their places in the shelves.
Nothing is disturbed. Nothing. I did not even know
you have been here."

"But that's . . . That's impossible," I stammered,
thinking he must be mistaken. "I was here on the
twenty-third of November. I remember it very
clearly. I left this room in a hurry. It was only later
that I remembered I had not switched off the lights
or replaced the books I had been using. Perhaps . . .
Perhaps someone came here over the weekend and
tidied everything up. One of the other members."

He shook his head.

"No," he said, "I think that was not so. No one
was here that weekend. Do you not remember that
we had a meeting in Glasgow? We had expected
you there. No one would have come in. Believe
me. No one."

My mind spun. Perhaps the whole incident had
been no more than a figment of my imagination,
the product of a fagged brain. But then I remembered the book in my briefcase, the reason for my

visit. How could it be there if I had not brought it away with me that night? I reached down and opened the case. The book was there, where I had put it. I drew it out and placed it on the desk in front of Jurczyk.

"I'm sorry," I said, "but when I left I must have put this book into my bag by mistake. I only found it there this morning when I was unpacking my papers. I realize you may have been worried about its loss. It seems extremely valuable."

He took it from me.

"There is no library mark," he said. "If it came from here it would have a label. On the spine."

"I found it over there," I said. "In the second stack. Behind some other books, stuck at the back of a shelf."

He frowned and opened the book. As his eyes fell on the title page, his expression changed. His cheeks, already pale, became ashen white. His eyes brightened with a mixture of fear and anger. I heard a sharp intake of breath, saw him clench his jaw. Then he slammed the book shut and pushed it away from him. He did not look at me, but sat staring at the table, as though struggling to regain control of himself. When at last he did look up, there was a fierce light in his eyes. His voice was quite changed, cold and accusatory in tone.

"You must tell me the truth," he said. "Where did you find this book? It was not found here. Where did it come from?"

Frightened and distressed by the abrupt change in the old man's manner, I stammered that I had indeed told him the truth, that the book had been lying under a layer of dust exactly where I had said.

"That is impossible," he said. "There has never been a copy of this book here. And even if it has been, it would never to be left in public. Such a things could not be allowed. I think you are a liar, Mr. Macleod. Perhaps worse than that. I would like you to leave. And take . . . that with you."

He pointed at the book, but refused to touch it. I picked it up, obeying him out of shock and embarrassment, and dropped it into my briefcase.

"Take it and get out of here," Jurczyk went on. "Do not come back. You will not be welcome here again."

I could not speak, could not bring a single word to my lips, whether of protest or denial. I understood my own innocence, but without knowing what crime I was being accused of, how could I find the words to refute it? I got to my feet awkwardly, knocking over the chair on which I had been sitting. Grabbing my still-open briefcase, I made for the door and hurried through it into the passage. Jurczyk came after me, limping to the opening in order to watch me go, as though afraid I might hide somewhere or leave the book behind me on the landing.

At the head of the stairs, I turned and looked back. Jurczyk stood framed in the open doorway, half in shadow, half in light, a look of mingled fear and anger fixed on his face like an ugly mask. I do not know what made me tear my eyes away and look along the passage to the pool of shadows at the foot of the stairs leading to the third floor. But as I looked I was certain that something moved there, furtively, without a sound. It was merely the flapping of a shadow within a shadow, but it seemed to fill the darkness with palpable terror. I turned and fled down the stairs.

BACK IN MY ROOMS, I filled a large glass with whisky and drank until my nerves felt calm again. What had Jurczyk meant by his outburst? The little book had clearly been familiar to him, it or its title, and it had frightened him badly. Thinking of my own experience, I did not have to guess what it was he had found disturbing. And I suspected that there might be more to the volume of spells than I, with my limited understanding of such matters, could possibly know. Given time, perhaps I could convince Jurczyk of my sincerity. But in the meantime, I would have to act alone.

The thought of spending the night alone with the *Matrix Aeternitatis* in my rooms was far from attractive. I could not leave it with anyone, possessed no bank deposit box in which to keep it, knew no one with whom I could talk about it. And I was in any case certain by now that the book was, in some sense that I could ill define, capable of evil. It went against everything I believed even to admit that such a thing could be possible, that an inanimate object could be capable of anything other than mere existence. But my own experience and Jurczyk's reaction had convinced me that to keep the book would be to risk consequences I could not as yet even guess at.

It took me a long time to make my mind up.

The book sat on my desk, drawing me to itself again and again. I felt a growing urge to open it, to see once more the drawing that had so alarmed me, that had formed the basis for such terrible dreams. But the longer I sat there, the more certain I became that the book must be destroyed. I guessed its rarity and knew it might be almost priceless. But with every minute that passed my impulse to destroy it grew more fixed.

At last I made my mind up. I got together wood and coals and laid them in my bedroom grate. In a little while, the coals caught, and I soon had a good fire going. I collected the book and hastened to throw it on the flames. It seemed almost to resist me. My hand shook as I held it over the grate, as though another force than my own will was trying to take charge. But I had come this far and was determined to be done with it. I threw the book onto the coals. It would not catch at first. But then, quite suddenly, it burst into flame all at once, as though soaked in petrol. Within a matter of minutes, it had been quite consumed. I poked the ashes that remained, breaking and scattering them. Some drifted up the chimney, flimsy white tissues lighter than smoke, others fell among the coals and were lost. I felt a great weight fall from me.

THAT NIGHT, I was kept awake by a constant scratching sound behind the wainscoting, as though rats or mice were scuttling in the walls.

Chapter 6

IT TOOK ME SOME DAYS to recover from the incident. The sight of old Jurczyk, whom I had previously known only as a kindhearted and affable man, shouting at me, telling me never to return, had been deeply upsetting.

I resumed work, but with a heavier heart than I had hoped. As the days passed and I put the incident at the Fraternity library behind me, my thoughts grew less perturbed. The scuttling sounds did not return the second night, nor any night after. The landlord must have put down rat poison, I thought. The shadows I had felt creeping up on me again had all but dispersed. From time to time, in the gray weather, I would feel uneasy walking past a dark opening or as I caught a sight of something moving against a window late at night. But for the most part I kept to crowded streets and strayed as little as possible beyond the reach of streetlights.

My research was hampered by my contretemps with Jurczyk. Such was the close-knittedness of the occult network in Edinburgh, I felt sure that word had by now gone round that little world to the effect that I was a thief or worse. I stuck with the more mainstream groups, people less likely to be in touch with the Fraternity of the Old Path or its members. But I soon grew frustrated, knowing that the richest information would come, not from people like these, but from the true adepts, those most deeply devoted to the magical arts. I thought now and then of contacting Jurczyk again, possibly by letter, in order to explain myself; but each time I put it off until it began to seem too late to retrieve the situation.

I had almost resigned myself to carrying out a less wide-ranging research program than I had originally envisaged, when matters took another unexpected turn. It was the middle of January, and I was in a pub in Bank Street. Ramsey McLean had asked me to join him for a drink. The invitation had been phrased quite casually—"a wee drink and a chance to catch up on news of Stornoway"—but I knew it was really to give him an opportunity to check up on my state of health. I knew that Iain was due to finish his classes later, and I was expecting him to join us when he was ready.

McLean brought two fine malt whiskies to the table, and we sat and talked like old times. He knew almost everyone in Stornoway, and had endless questions to ask about this or that household, about the children and grandchildren of neighbors.

When an hour or so had passed, the doctor finished his third whisky and set the empty glass on the table.

"I have to go," he said. "Evening surgery starts in half an hour. Andrew, you're greatly improved. Keep taking the herbal drink. When the bottle's empty, pop into the surgery for a new one. I'll give you a once-over. By the looks of you, you'll be in top form by the spring."

I said I would stay on to wait for Iain. McLean shook hands and left, and I went to the bar for a soft drink. I had barely returned to my table when a man sat down next to me.

"Andrew Macleod," he said. "Where on earth have you been hiding?"

I turned awkwardly, almost spilling my drink. For a moment I did not recognize him, for his face was not one I associated with the place or the time of day. His name was Duncan Mylne, an advocate, like half the other customers in the pub. We were near the law courts here.

He and I had met a few times at meetings of the Fraternity of the Old Path, of which he was a long-standing member. I had been particularly intrigued by him, for he did not fit the stereotype of the cult adherent in terms of social class, intellect, education, or anything else, as far as I could see. We had spoken at length once or twice, and I had marked him down as someone I should get to know better. At the same time, I had been a little wary of him, fearing that, with his unusually incisive mind—a mind long practiced in sniffing out incon-sistencies and nailing lies—he would see through my flimsy cover.

I shook hands and told him I had been ill.

"I'm sorry to hear that," he said. He was a man of about fifty, in excellent physical shape, conserva-tively but expensively dressed, and well groomed. He spoke with the upper-class accent of a Scot who had attended the public school Fettes College and taken a first degree at Oxford before studying law at St. Andrews.

"You were becoming a familiar face at our meetings," he went on. "The Fraternity can always do with fresh blood, and for my own part a little intelligent conversation never goes amiss. I had high hopes of receiving you for initiation before long. Are you better now?"

"Yes . . . yes, quite better," I stammered. He made me nervous in some way, I do not know how. As though his gaze penetrated me, as though his thoughts reached beneath my skin.

"Well, then, I trust it won't be long before we see you back at Ainslie Place."

I reddened, not knowing if Jurczyk had spoken to him about me or not.

"I'm afraid—" I started, coming to an abrupt halt almost at once. I decided there was nothing for it but to confront the matter head-on. "Look, I may as well tell you, if you haven't heard already, that I had a . . . spot of unpleasantness with your Mr. Jurczyk. I think he suspected me of trying to steal a book from the library."

"Did you?"

"No, of course not, I . . . "

"Then I don't see why you should make a thing of it."

"It was just . . . He was very angry. I thought he might have spoken to other members."

"Jurczyk? No, he couldn't have." He paused. There was a trace of whisky on his lower lip. His look was disconcerting. "I take it you know about Jurczyk?"

There was something in his voice that made my heart shiver.

"Know?"

"What happened to him."

"No, I've heard nothing. What? . . . "

"He was found dead a couple of weeks ago. Margaret Laurie found him in the library one Thursday morning when she went in to type some letters. He'd been there overnight, so the doctor said."

My heart had stopped shivering. I was cold everywhere now, just cold, as if it had become winter inside me.

"How . . . how did he die?"

"Heart attack. So they say. Margaret said she thought something might have frightened him. She told me his face was contorted, as though he had tried to cry out. But that's not unusual in a heart attack. I've listened to enough medical reports in my time. Pain, I told her, not fear. That's what made him look like that."

I put down my drink. I was feeling sick. He was lying there, Jurczyk, I could see him on the library floor. Crying out.

"When was this exactly?" I asked.

He looked at me oddly.

"When? I'm not sure. Early this month, a week or so after New Year."

"Could it have been the eighth?"

"It could have been. Yes, I think it was. What's wrong?"

"That . . . was the day I had the argument with him. You don't think? . . . "

He smiled reassuringly.

"Oh, I'm sure not. He was an old man. A sick man. It was just a matter of time. You shouldn't worry about that. Put it out of your head."

I looked up and caught sight of Iain on the other side of the lounge, coming toward me. As was usual when he was lecturing, he did not wear his dog collar. For some reason it relieved me that he did not. As he came up and greeted me, Mylne got down from his stool and picked up his coat.

"I've got to be going," he said. "I have a big case to mug up on before tomorrow morning. Andrew, you must come to a meeting soon. I'll pick you up some evening, we'll go together."

And then he was gone.

THAT NIGHT, I started dreaming again, and each night after for a week. Each night the same dream, but always a little more; and with the lengthening of the dream, an intensification of dread.

On the first night, I dreamed I was back on Lewis, in Stornoway, with a great wind and a black sky, the sea in torment, raised high by the storm, leafless winter trees bent and snapping. I was running through darkened streets, the doors and windows of the houses shut fast, no light shining in any of them, as though I was running through a city of the dead.

Suddenly, at the end of the street, a great black church rose up out of nowhere, grim and vast and silent, like no church I had ever seen on the island or elsewhere. As my eyes fell on it, I awoke with a start, its black shape still before my eyes and the sound of the wind rushing still in my ears.

On the second and successive nights, I ran again and again through those dark, silent streets, closer and closer to the door of the black church, a door that reared high above me, dwarfing me. On the third night, I pushed it open and saw for the first time its cathedrallike interior, forbidding and dark, lit only here and there with a few stunted candles. Just as I awoke again, the door slammed behind me, cutting off the wind, and I could hear from within a strange, mournful sound, as of many voices rising and falling in unison.

By the next night, things had begun to escalate. This time, when I opened the door and looked inside, I could hear the sound of the deep-throated chanting, rising to fill the vast spaces of the vault. As I listened, I thought at first that what I could hear were the metrical psalms of my boyhood. The swelling voices lifted in dirgelike strains, mournful, filled with a dark yearning, and I was sure I had come upon a great congregation of the people of Lewis, perhaps a gathering of generations of the island's dead in a dark cathedral beyond the con-

fines of the real world. But as I listened more
closely, I realized that the words were not Gaelic,
but in a language I had never before heard.

Night after night I returned to that place in my
dreams, listening to the strange chanting, straining
to make out the physical details of the vast chamber
in which I stood. My eyes seemed to grow rapidly
accustomed to the dark, and soon I could make out
the figures of the congregation standing with their
backs to me, facing a dimly lit altar at the far end of
the building. Their voices were deep and sonorous,
but they neither swayed nor moved their heads as
they chanted. Out of sight, a priest sang out the
verses of a liturgy unknown to me. Strange shapes,
barely visible in the pale candlelight, lurked in the
shadows of the walls all about, statues or gargoyles.
Something about their outlines made me glad I
could not see them more clearly.

Each night, my feelings of unease mounted. I
knew without having been told that in the shadows
some unknown menace waited. The deeper I was
carried into the body of the church, the greater
grew my sense of foreboding. The volume of the
chanting rose constantly, and with it the certainty
that something unpleasant lurked ahead of me. As I
drew closer to the congregation, I saw that they
were dressed in white robes that fell shroudlike
from shoulder to heel, and that at their feet scuttled
thin white shapes, larger than rats and more agile.

One night, as I stood filled with dread at the
heart of the black church, the chanting stopped
abruptly. A chilling silence filled the dark spaces.
For what seemed an age, I stood in the silence and

darkness, reluctantly staring at the robed figures in front of me. Then, as if at a command, they started to turn where they stood, to face me where I waited, transfixed, behind them. As my eyes fell on their faces, I woke screaming in pure terror.

I did what I could to avoid sleep the following night. The thought of what I might see made me dread unconsciousness. I drank cup after cup of coffee and played music through the night. But I could not hold out. Just before dawn, I became drowsy, and in the end slipped into a deep sleep. When I awoke, it was early afternoon. To my surprise, I realized that my sleep had been untroubled. Untroubled, yet not normal. For I dreamed no dreams at all.

Chapter 7

DUNCAN MYLNE CAME FOR ME on the evening following the last dream. It did not then occur to me to ask how he knew my address. He arrived unannounced, taking my presence for granted, never questioning that I might be ready to be collected and taken to the Fraternity. There was a presumption about him, an air of someone who does not even imagine that he may be denied. I made no objection, however. It was raining, and I was grateful for the lift. And, although I did not feel quite easy in his presence, I was sure a better acquaintance with him would prove rewarding.

The meeting was unexceptional. Watching the initiates perform their dreary rites, I could not help letting my eyes stray more than once to Mylne. He seemed bored with the whole business, like someone who goes through a ritual for the sake of habit or appearance, rather than with any inner conviction. Perhaps, I thought, this is no more than the public facade and there are other rites reserved for an inner circle to which he and a few others belong. That would explain why a man of his intelligence might put up with the banality of this little clique and the theatricality of its performances, week after week.

Afterward, driving back through a slow drizzle that had set in for the night, we chatted of everyday matters, as though returning from a play for which neither of us had much cared. But as we came into the High Street, he turned and spoke in a more earnest voice.

"Andrew," he said, "I feel we need to talk. Can you spare half an hour to have a drink? I keep some very good whisky in my rooms. They're just down here, next to Parliament House."

I might very well have suspected this was no more than a ruse to seduce me. Mylne was, I knew, unmarried, and he had the slightly concealed manner of a homosexual whose first encounters with other men had predated the liberalization of the law; but I did not think he had designs on me, at least not of the sexual kind. I accepted his invitation readily, believing it an opportunity to probe a little more deeply into the nature of his affiliation with the Fraternity and the extent of his involvement in occult matters.

His rooms were, like his dress, understated and expensive. Above a black marble fireplace hung an oil painting of a man in legal costume dating from the last century. On either side of it stood two large bookcases packed with richly bound volumes. The main chamber was more like a living room than working quarters.

He took my coat and hung it in a small closet in the hall. Within minutes he had a fire going in the hearth. I was instructed to make myself comfortable in a deep, damask-upholstered armchair while Mylne busied himself with glasses and whisky.

"No ice," he said, handing me my glass. "Don't even ask me to add water. This stuff has to be taken neat."

When I sipped it I understood: any whisky I had had before was paint stripper by comparison.

"Well," he said, settling himself in the chair facing mine, "tell me about this business with the book."

"There's not much to tell," I said, knowing I could never reveal what had really happened.

"Nevertheless. I'm interested. It seems to have upset you."

I made up a story about how I had been taken ill suddenly while working in the library and, on recovering, had found a volume in my briefcase that must have slipped in that same evening and been forgotten.

"What was the title of this slippery book?" he asked.

"I . . . I can't quite remember. It was a copy of Walker, I think, or Crowley's *Book of the Law.*"

Mylne gave a mock shudder and sipped his whisky.

"Not that awful thing, surely. I thought you had more sense. 'Do what thou wilt shall be the whole of the Law.' Stuff and nonsense."

"I feel I have to read everything," I said.

"Yes, of course. That is only natural at your stage. But there are limits. Crowley is one of them. You require some guidance. Otherwise you will waste your time on the works of charlatans. Leave Crowley to adolescent boys. You have more serious work ahead of you."

I sensed that I was on the verge of the breakthrough I had been hoping for all this time, that I was about to breach another level in the occult hierarchy.

"That's easy enough for you to say," I retorted, hoping to draw him out yet further. "But where is this guidance to come from? I read what I can, attend rituals and lectures, speak with anyone who will spare me a moment. But as far as I can see, I'm on my own."

He looked at me oddly, then set his glass down on a low table.

"Why do you come to the meetings of the Fraternity? What are you looking for?"

"Knowledge," I said, hoping it might not sound too banal. It was, at least, an approximation of the truth. "I'm in search of knowledge."

"Every Tom, Dick, or Harry is after knowledge," he replied. "You are not ordinary. I want to know what it is you seek that the ordinary man does not even guess at."

Had I not by then read all round the subject, I might not have happened on the answer he sought.

But there was one word that I had kept returning to in book after book, and I sensed it was what he was looking for from me.

"Mastery," I said. "Real knowledge and final mastery."

He smiled, not altogether attractively, and I knew I had said the right thing.

"Do you think you will find it among the Fraternity of the Old Path?" he asked.

I shook my head. I knew by now roughly where this was leading.

"No," I said. "But everyone has to begin somewhere."

"That's very honest of you," he said. "Tell me, is the library at Ainslie Place adequate for your researches?"

I shook my head again.

"It was to begin with, but not now. The books I really want are not available. I have tried in the National Library, but either they do not have them or they will not let me see them."

"Oh, they have them all right. But they are kept under lock and key. You would need very important friends indeed to be given permission even to glance at them. But perhaps I can help you. I have an extensive library. Not this," he said, indicating the rows of leather-bound volumes behind us. "This is just part of my family collection. I brought them here after my parents died. But my real library I keep at home. It includes several items I think you will find of interest. Unfortunately, they are extremely valuable. You will understand if I do not offer to lend them to you. But I can bring a few of them here. I am often here in the evenings myself, preparing briefs. You are free to come when you like."

He paused.

"Many of the most important volumes are in foreign languages. Which are you fluent in?"

"Latin," I said, "and Greek. I studied both of them for A-level. My father was originally a classicist. Gaelic, of course—but I expect that's of no use. French. A little German."

"Hebrew?"

I shook my head.

"A pity. There are one or two interesting treatises. And I will assume you know no Arabic."

Again I shook my head, thinking this time of the book I had found in Ainslie Place, translated from Arabic into Latin.

"The Arabs taught the medieval masters much of what they knew. Jabir ibn Hayyan became famous as Geber, and an entire corpus of alchemical writings appeared in his name. A book called *Picatrix* was translated into Spanish and then Latin from an Arabic text called the *Rutbat al-Hakim*: it influenced everyone from Peter of Abano to Campanella. The Baghdadi Abu Ma'shar al-Balkhi was widely known in Europe as Albumazar, the greatest of astrologers.

"Later, when you are more advanced, it will pay you to learn Arabic at least. However, the Latin and Greek are extremely fortunate: I had not expected them. You will need tuition in the technical terms, then we can start on some simpler texts. Come here tomorrow at seven. We will have a light dinner, then your instruction can begin."

"And the Fraternity?" I asked, for I needed to know whether this was just an offer to improve my reading, or whether that was only the beginning. I had my answer straight away.

"Oh, forget about them. They are of no importance. You are destined for greatness, Andrew. I can sense it. But you are not ready yet. Read the books I give you. Ask whatever questions you like. And when the time comes, I shall introduce you to some friends of mine who know what those fools in Ainslie Place do not even guess at."

WE TALKED TILL LATE, and when I walked home it had stopped raining. Mylne had asked what sort of work I did, and I had told him I was studying for my doctorate in sociology, writing a thesis on Durkheim. He had no reason to disbelieve me, and the fiction allowed me some latitude. Nevertheless, that night when I got home, the first thing I did was to put all my notebooks and the documentation relating to my research into a cupboard, in case he should pay me a visit and stumble across them. I disliked the need for secrecy, but it seemed essential to me, all the more so in view of Mylne's promise to introduce me to friends who, I guessed, would not wish to see their activities brought into the light of day.

In the days and weeks that followed, I began to see more of Mylne and less and less of Iain and Harriet. On more than one occasion, I broke an engagement with Iain in order to hurry back to Duncan's rooms for tuition. My seminars grew increasingly complex and riddled with obscurities. One by one, both students and staff began to absent themselves. Iain told me there had been mutterings in the corridors after more than one seminar. My material was growing far too esoteric, he said, too much detached from sociological or any other reality. I told him to mind his own business.

Duncan brought heaps of books to his rooms. Together, we read voraciously, almost every night. We began with texts with which I was familiar, before moving to more recondite volumes. They were heavy books bound in thick leather, as daunting to lift as to read. Their pages were stained and curled with age, their heavy type cramped and difficult to understand at first. Most of them dated from the sixteenth and seventeenth centuries, but one or two were older and immensely rare.

Mylne's explanations shed light into the darkest corners, and I began to understand how puerile my grasp of things had been until now. With his help, I mastered the intricacies of the medieval Latin used in magical and alchemical lore, and started to tackle the principal texts of ritual magic. When I first saw them, I was astonished by some of the titles he laid before me. Books of which I had heard no more than the name, incunabula of which only three or four copies had survived.

At the end of each session, he would teach me a little Arabic, and I bought a grammar to study at home. Gradually, we had started to read simple texts. And when we read Latin translations from that language, he would often refer me back to the original, correcting or improving the translator's version.

He showed me how to build a pentacle and construct talismans for both protection and invocation. I soon saw that my earlier efforts had been of no greater merit than a child's attempt to build a dwelling with broken twigs and mud. By now, my interest in the occult had passed from the academic to the personal. My earlier researches seemed to me nothing more than arid intellectual games. I wanted real knowledge now, knowledge I could taste, knowledge with which to accomplish something more than the construction of theories. It was as I had said: I wanted mastery.

UNDER HIS TUITION, I became proficient in the rudiments of the craft. Once, unwittingly, I spoke of our mutual interest in the "black arts." He grew angry and corrected me at once.

"They are neither black nor white," he said. "Leave morality to the Church. Magic transcends common dichotomy. It has deeper purposes. A spell may be used to kill a saint or overthrow a tyrant, a charm will protect a murderer as soon as a priest."

He took down a medieval grimoire from the top shelf and opened it at a section dealing with "Spelles and Incantaytiones for the Procuring Harme to Thyne Enemie."

"There are spells here," he said, "which, if correctly recited will kill or injure a man. They are infallible, I assure you. The most that is needed is a lock of the victim's hair or an article of his clothing to be his representative. The hat or the glove is nothing. The spell is nothing. What counts is the will of the conjuror, his determination that his victim shall fall ill or die. If his intention is pure, what follows, however evil it might seem in the eyes of the multitude, will also be pure."

"Even if harm is done to a good man?"

"You cannot judge that until you possess the knowledge of a master."

"Have you ever used spells like these?"

He returned the book to its high place.

"I have done all manner of things," he said. "When you are ready, we will study these spells together. And now, it's time for supper."

ONE AFTERNOON IN SPRING, I was at home reading when there was a knock on my door. I opened it to find Harriet standing on the landing. She did not ask if she could come in, but pushed past me and headed straight for the living room. I closed the door and followed her.

"Harriet, I don't know what you think you're—"

She spun, facing me.

"I won't waste your precious time, Andrew, don't worry. I can see you have plenty of reading to catch up on."

The room was cluttered with books, items from the university library, a few from my own small collection, and one or two modern volumes lent me by Duncan.

"That fact is, Iain and I are very worried about you," she went on, not giving me a chance to interrupt. "We were frightened by what happened to you before Christmas. You were very ill, I don't think you know how much. McLean told us you were heading for a complete breakdown. He warned you about overworking, but here you are a few months later, pushing yourself harder than ever. You've got no time for your friends, you've given up on Iain's seminars, all you seem to do is sit with your nose stuck in books that were consigned to the bin centuries ago. It might not be so bad if you were doing serious academic work; but this . . . "

She gestured at the books all round her. Her arm seemed weary, her face pitying.

"I understand this better than any academic," I retorted. "I'm not just scraping the surface now, I'm underneath, I'm learning how to connect with the essence of what I read about. Can Iain or his colleagues say as much? Can you?"

"I doubt we can. But I doubt any of us would want to connect with the world you're letting yourself get sucked into. Andrew, we are concerned. We want to help you, Iain and I. This man Mylne—for heaven's sake, Andrew, he has the worst reputation. Iain has asked around—people in the church, people in the law, people at the university. Mylne's notorious. If he weren't so damned clever, he'd have been in jail years ago."

"I'd take care, Harriet. Duncan Mylne is a friend of mine. A good friend. I've learned things from him you'd scarcely imagine."

"He's a dangerous man, Andrew. Look at you. You're half in a daze. You can't do your job, you're losing weight, you're heading for another collapse. He's destroyed people before this, and he'll destroy you if you let him."

"Is this all you've come for, Harriet? What about Iain? Hasn't he got the courage to say all this to my face?"

"Iain doesn't know I'm here. He'd never have agreed to my coming, he doesn't want me mixed up in this. But we're both worried sick. Why don't you come and stay with us for a few days, just to talk things over? Iain can introduce you to some of his friends who know about Mylne. They can—"

"I think you'd better leave, Harriet." I took her elbow, started propelling her toward the door. "If this is all you have to say, you've been wasting your time."

There were tears in her eyes, but they were thrown away on me. I was like someone watching himself from a distance, quite uninvolved, quite untouched. Duncan had taught me how to master my emotions, how to stop them from interfering with my main enterprise, my quest for ‾arcane knowledge.

Harriet left, pleading with me to reconsider. I scarcely noticed. By the time I had shut the door and gone back to the book I had been reading, she had been all but forgotten.

I DREAMED OF CATRIONA THAT NIGHT, a strange dream, without beginning or end. She stood in a long, dark street, weeping and calling my name. It was a foreign place, full of high buildings built from mud. Shuttered windows patched the walls on all sides. From time to time a door opened and closed. The doorway was black. I could hear feet walking on stones nearby. I wanted to run to Catriona, to hold and kiss her and tell her all was well, but I could not move. That is all I remember.

Chapter 8

I VERY NEARLY BETRAYED MYSELF to Mylne through sheer carelessness, a few days after Harriet's visit. He came, as he often did in those days, to see me at my flat. It had become his custom to call out of the blue, as though to surprise me or, as I now believe, spy on me. I would usually offer him a drink, grateful for the relief of his company after a day's solitary reading. Quite often we would listen together to a piece of classical music, and sometimes he would stay and I would prepare a light meal. It was his means of getting to know me better, to observe me in my own environment—I almost said, my natural habitat.

That evening, we ate and drank and talked until quite late. The subject of our conversation was the islands, which he told me he had never visited.

For a man of his urbanity, he seemed unduly interested in Lewis and the life we led there. My home seemed unbelievably remote to me now, like a place I had read about yet never gone to.

I had, as I have mentioned, hidden away any books or papers that might inadvertently reveal the true nature of my research, and I was accustomed to letting Duncan go where he wanted in the flat. As he was leaving, however, his eye fell on an envelope I had left lying on the hall table. He picked it up.

"This is addressed to Dr. Andrew Macleod," he said. "I thought you said you were still working on your thesis."

I felt a chill go through me. There was something in his tone that warned me the wrong answer would cause trouble, though I could not guess quite how. I realized for the first time that, much as I admired Duncan Mylne, I also feared him. If he knew that I had concealed the true nature of my original research from him, he might very well vent his anger on me.

"I am," I said. "This happens all the time. I've had letters addressed to me as professor before now. Not everyone understands the system. They think that, if you're studying for a doctorate, you're already a doctor."

He laughed and put the envelope down.

"I know the problem," he said. "The common herd has little enough understanding of anything outside their limited horizons. I'm often called a solicitor, once I was made a judge."

He went away, though I could not be sure how

reassured he had been by my explanation. I went through everything after that, removing all traces of my other life for fear he should stumble on them. And yet, in a sense, it mattered little now. My thirst for the knowledge whose promise Mylne held out to me so alluringly was no longer a pretence to mask an academic's enquiries, but wholly genuine, a self-engendered passion that would allow no hindrance. I feared not so much exposure as the loss of the opportunity to carry my new investigations to their proper conclusion.

In the weeks that followed, my apprehensions were gradually laid to rest. Duncan proved no less attentive than before, there were no awkward questions, life continued much as ever. He never invited me to his home, never let our relationship become an ordinary friendship. I quickly learned that I was his apprentice, and that he possessed authority over me. He never stated this in words, never presumed upon it; but as time passed it became the core around which our comings and goings circled.

IAIN CAME TO SEE ME on a blustery day at the end of April. A cold wind had come in from the Firth, turning an otherwise pleasant spring day into something better suited to the tail end of autumn.

"I have to speak with you, Andrew," he said as I opened the door. "Please don't shut me out."

I let him in and said I would put on a pot of tea. I could guess what lay ahead: a tirade against Duncan Mylne, dire warnings about the company I was keeping, advice about my health.

He was in the living room when I returned with the tea. His coat and scarf lay across the back of a chair, about the only free space available. He was in clerical dress. I gave him his mug, plain tea with milk and sugar. Duncan had introduced me to China teas, and I had prepared a pot of choice Formosa Oolong for myself. I passed Iain a plate of biscuits.

"Chocolate Olivers?" he said, raising his eyebrows. "You didn't pick these off a shelf in Tesco."

"I was given them," I said. "Look, Iain—"

He got there before me.

"Don't worry," he said. "I'm not here to preach. Harriet's already spoken to me about her visit. I could have told her it would be a waste of time. I'm sorry we don't see as much of you as we did, but you know we're always there if you'd like to visit us. I can't promise you Chocolate Olivers, but—"

"I've been busy," I said, making a pointless apology.

"There's no need," said Iain. "I can see that. And I won't pretend I'm not deeply worried about it all. But I haven't called on my own behalf or Harriet's. James Fergusson asked me to drop by. He needs to see you, but he doesn't think you'd take to his calling in out of the blue."

He paused and sipped his tea.

"I haven't seen Fergusson in a little while," I said. "He's written to me a few times, but the truth is I have no time for the man."

"That's fair enough, I don't like him either. But the fact is, he's your boss, and he has a right to know what you've been up to. The university pays your salary, and it expects results. Look, Andrew, you may as well know—Fergusson is not going to recommend the renewal of your contract after July. And I don't think he's prepared to write a favorable report either. I don't think you're going to find it easy to get a new post, not unless you do something drastic between now and the summer."

"I've been working like a slave. I—"

"You haven't been doing the work you were contracted to do. What you did at first was excellent, and we all appreciated it. But you've allowed yourself to get sidetracked."

"It's research all the same."

"No, Andrew, it's not. Not any longer. You've buried yourself so deeply in this thing, you can't see clearly any longer. But I promised not to preach to you, so I won't. I'll just pass on Fergusson's message and leave you. It's up to you what you do about it."

Perhaps I give the impression that I remained cool throughout this conversation. Inwardly, though, I was torn. I wanted to reassure Iain that I still valued his friendship and that of Harriet, that I did not want to lose them. But something held me back. It was, I think, fear of the high price I might have to pay in order to regain Iain's trust.

Iain drained his mug and set it down on the floor beside him.

"Andrew," he said, "I'm sorry if this seems tiresome, but there is something I want to tell you. It won't take long, and I promise I'll go when I've finished."

There was a knock at the door. Glancing at the clock, my heart sank: it could only be Duncan. I went to the hall and opened the front door. Duncan was standing a few feet away.

The moment he came in, he guessed something was wrong. He wore a warm overcoat and soft kid gloves. His cheeks were red and his hair tossed from the wind. I felt weak beside him.

"What's the matter, Andrew? You seem on edge."

I shook my head. At that moment, Iain appeared in the doorway of the living room, his coat over one arm.

Duncan noticed the dog collar, I could tell. They looked at each other like old enemies meeting on neutral ground. When he stepped forward, I noticed that Iain kept his distance from Duncan.

"I'm on my way," he said. "Thanks for the tea, Andrew. I'll give James Fergusson your message. Remember to get in touch if you have a moment."

"I will," I said, then, in an effort to ease things, I introduced them.

"Duncan, this is Iain Gillespie. He's a lecturer at New College. Iain's been a great help to me with some of my work."

"I'm sure," said Duncan, stripping off a glove and stretching out his hand. "Duncan Mylne, a friend of Andrew's." He paused. "Haven't we met before? Your name seems familiar."

"We may have bumped into one another; Edinburgh's a small town. And your name is familiar enough to me, Mr. Mylne. Now, perhaps you'll excuse me. I have a seminar to run."

He thanked me again and left, turning once as he went through the door to wave good-bye to me. His face seemed troubled.

"A man of the cloth," said Duncan, going ahead of me into the living room. "I didn't know you had such exotic taste in friends."

"Iain's not a friend," I lied. It hurt to hear myself saying it. "But he's a good sociologist of religion, an expert on Berger."

I was flustered. While Duncan settled himself, I tidied up the tea things and hurried them out of the room.

That night, for the first time since our acquaintance began, we spoke of personal matters. He told me that his father had been a doctor, and that his family's wealth had come from his grandfather, a cloth importer who had traded with the Levant and North Africa. He had never married, but there had been several women in his life, by none of whom had he had children. That was something he now regretted. He had, he said, more than just material possessions to pass on to an heir. It pained him to think that the knowledge and arcane wisdom he had gathered in his lifetime should die with him.

He seemed a little afraid of death, he would not say why. It was in part that dread of severance from his own hard-earned heritage. But I sensed that he had also experienced loss and, in spite of his occult learning, could find no belief to assure him of reunion in another life. Those, at least, were my first thoughts. It was only later that I came to understand that his fear came, not from lack of knowledge, but from too much.

He did, however, tell me that both his parents were dead, his father in a shooting accident, his mother of cancer. It was that which prompted me to speak to him of Catriona, though I had at first vowed never to do so. He listened to my story with sympathy and, I thought, the sensitivity of one who has known what it is to lose someone near.

"Where do you think she is now?" he asked, quite abruptly, when I had finished talking. "At peace, as your clerical friend might put it? In heaven? In hell?"

"Oh, I could never think that," I said. "I can't believe that anyone could be condemned to hell. The whole concept is totally unjust. And Catriona . . . No, I could never think that."

"But you would like to see her again."

"I have no hope of that," I said. "I can't believe in an afterlife of any sort."

"Then the Reverend Gillespie has had no luck with you?"

I flushed.

"I've already told you, I scarcely know him. He's never spoken to me about his beliefs."

"Oh, I've little doubt. They've grown subtle nowadays. But not even your desire to see Catriona once more can convince you of the possibility?"

I shook my head.

"And yet," he said, choosing his words with great care, "and yet I wonder if you are right. We have already spoken of other realities. In time, you will learn much more of them. Your Catriona may not be so far away as you think." He looked past me a fraction, as though staring at something or someone behind my shoulder. "Who knows? She may be with you now. Perhaps she has never left you."

I could not help myself. I glanced round, looking in the direction indicated by him. But, of course, there was no one there. He laughed softly.

"It's time I was away, Andrew. We've talked enough for tonight. Come to my rooms tomorrow. I have a new book for you to read."

I HAD THE DREAM that night again, the dream of Catriona. This time she was not alone, this time a second figure stood beside her. Something made me think it was Iain, but the face was in darkness, the figure itself blurred.

I was wakened the next morning by the telephone. It was Iain.

"Andrew, I'm sorrow to disturb you. It's nothing very important. Just that I thought I left my scarf at your place yesterday. Could you check if it's there?"

I looked everywhere I could think of, but it was nowhere to be seen.

"I can't find it Iain," I said. "It was with you when you arrived, I remember that, so you must have taken it away with you. Did you go anywhere after my place?"

"No, I came straight home. There was no seminar. Well, it's very odd, then. If you do come across it, perhaps you'll give me a ring. You know the one, purple, blue, and white stripes."

"Iain . . . " I halted, not certain what it was I had wanted to say.

"What is it, Andrew?"

I did know after all what had been on my tongue. But I could not say it.

"Nothing," I said instead, "it's nothing. I'll get in touch. I promise. Very soon."

He said good-bye, and I was alone again in my silent rooms with my books all around me. Or perhaps . . . I thought of what Duncan had said the night before. Perhaps I was not alone after all.

Chapter

9

THAT EVENING, AFTER OUR STUDIES, Duncan grew expansive again. He asked more about my family and my life on Lewis, then came back again to the subject of Catriona, in which he seemed particularly interested. At his request, I had brought some photographs, which I showed him: he was the first person I had allowed to see them since Catriona's death. He looked through them slowly, saying nothing. His fingers caressed the surface of each one gently, with a soft rotating motion. He whispered something beneath his breath, then handed them back to me.

"What did you say just now?" I asked.

He shook his head.

"Not now," he said. "Later. When it is time."

I did not ask what he meant. I had learned

when to keep silent. I knew that he *was* interested in Catriona and in what she had meant to me. More than ever, I became sure that he had suffered a similar tragedy and that he would in time come to speak of it to me.

As I put the photographs back in my briefcase, he asked a curious question.

"Do you have any photographs of her grave?"

I shook my head.

"It . . . never occurred to me to take any," I said. "It's not really something I like to be reminded of."

"But you visit it."

"On anniversaries and the like—yes, I do."

"The next time you go, take a photograph for me. I would like to see where she is buried."

Had he asked it months or even weeks before, I would have found the request morbid, perhaps repulsive. But I meekly said I would and put the matter out of my mind.

His next question was almost as strange.

"Do you have a current passport?"

"I expect so. Yes, it doesn't run out for a year or two."

"Good, very good. In that case, I want you to make yourself available to travel this summer."

"Travel? Where to?"

He folded his hands on his lap and looked at me intently.

"I make a journey every summer to Morocco. There are people there I have come to know, extraordinary people whose knowledge I value above any other. Holy men, marabouts, masters of the wisdom you and I have been studying.

"This year, I want you to accompany me. We shall travel together to Fez and Marrakesh, then into the deep south. You will see things you have only dreamed of, meet people you would never meet in a lifetime."

"I . . . I don't think I can afford it. After June I have no income whatever. . . . "

He shook his head.

"Let me take care of everything. It's not an expensive country. I want you to come with me this year because I think it is time. You have made remarkable progress in your studies, but you have still only touched the externals. In Morocco you will begin to taste the fruit. And then you will be ready for Claremont Place."

"What's there?" I asked.

"Just a place where I meet now and then with friends. There are people I want to introduce you to. But as I told you before, you are not yet ready. Morocco will help prepare you."

It took little to persuade me in the end. I would, after all, be virtually penniless from the end of June, and I had already started wondering what would happen if I had to abandon Edinburgh and my studies with Duncan. Now, it seemed, I need worry no longer. All would be taken care of. I was in safe hands.

Early in June, I made a special visit to Glasgow, to the cemetery where Catriona was buried. I brought a small camera with me and took several photographs. The stone had a neglected air. Catriona's parents lived in Aberdeen now, and they visited the grave infrequently. I cleaned it as well as I could, but it seemed no less dismal to me.

When I showed the photographs to Duncan, he seemed pleased. He asked if he could keep one and, although I thought it strange, I said he could.

WE LEFT AT THE BEGINNING OF JULY, flying from London to Casablanca. Even with the summer sun upon it, Casablanca was revoltingly dull, a steaming metropolis with neither the glamour nor the cunning of a true Oriental city. Duncan saw the disappointment on my face that first day when, coming from our hotel in the squalid heart of the town, we set off to find a café to drink mint tea and sweet almond milk.

"There is nothing for us here," he said. "Just a day to rest in, to get our bearings."

I remember nothing now of Casablanca but constant noise and petrol fumes, gray buildings, weary people, a sense of drab monotony everywhere. We ate that evening in the restaurant of our hotel. I slept heavily, as though drugged.

The next day we traveled by train to Rabat, the capital. I was to learn, throughout that long summer, that Morocco was not a country to be entered all at once or apprehended in a single week. I came to it by slow degrees, from city to city, guided at all times by Duncan. It was not one place, but a landscape of the imagination. I saw it in my mind as much as with my eyes. People and towns were veils that had to be stripped away until there was nothing left but pure vision.

It is hard to write from memory the details of those months. I think now that I must have been delirious or drugged much of the time. Duncan had not brought me to Morocco in order to open my mind, but to destroy my soul. I followed him like a lost spirit into a Hades he conjured up for me out of its cities and deserts. He was my Virgil, stepping ahead of me into an underworld whose pathways only he could follow.

In Rabat, we spent days obtaining permits for travel into the interior. There was a low-grade war in the western Sahara, there had been trouble on the border with Algeria, and the government, obstructive at the best of times, was thoroughly uncooperative. Duncan left me in our hotel or at the Café Maure while he hunted down his papers and stamps at this ministry or that. It cost him a good deal in patience and much more in money spent in bribes, but he was good-humored about it.

A young man was sent to my room twice a day to practice Moroccan Arabic with me. He had a soft face, like a girl's, and perpetually sad eyes. His name was Idris. Our time together was mostly spent speaking of the simplest things, using the few words I knew or could guess at from the classical. But once or twice he broke into his clumsy student's English and spoke to me of himself and the numerous sadnesses of his life. I think he expected me to sleep with him, but I shied away from that, as I had always done.

I felt lonely most of the time. The sunlight on the river facing the café was blinding during the long hot days. At night, when it was cool, Duncan and I would sit in a small courtyard scented with bougainvillea and read crabbed Arabic texts by the light of an oil lamp. When we finished, the moon would be high above our heads, almost lost among the branches of tall plane trees, and there would be silence everywhere, and stars across the night sky.

We moved to Tangier, to a small house in the rue Ben Raisouli, near the Petit Socco. The house belonged to Roger Villiers, an old friend of Duncan's and a long-established inhabitant of the city. An Englishman, he had moved to Tangier in the thirties and had known it in the heyday of the international set. He had introduced Paul Bowles to selected groups of Moroccan writers, had smoked kif with William Burroughs, and had even enjoyed a brief affair with Barbara Hutton, the Woolworth heiress.

Speaking of those things, he could be wickedly funny. He was an old man who had long known his own value and, for that matter, the precise value of everyone he had ever met. Not in monetary terms, but in respect of what they represented, or who or what they knew, or how well read they were.

I think that, on the whole, he despised me, but put up with me for Duncan's sake. My stilted academic learning was worth nothing to him, and my knowledge of the occult was, I gradually discovered, but a tiny fragment of his own. He showed not the slightest interest in me or my experiences. I hardly blame him for that. He was, after all, more than a mere man of the world. Without leaving his little house, he had met all the best people, uncovered all the most coveted secrets.

In the evenings, there were small gatherings attended by members of Villiers's set, who numbered a couple of dozen at most. Three or four would come each evening. None were of my age or even close to it, and several were so advanced in years as to seem like relics of another civilization. They had rotten teeth and sagging cheeks, set off by that aloof charm the very rich retain when all else is gone. They spoke of friends in Paris or Nice, of relatives in New York, of salons in Rome.

They were all Americans or Europeans, and their conversation was conducted in a mixture of English and French, interspersed with snatches of Moroccan Arabic. There were drinks in tall glasses on the tables beside the banquettes on which they sat, and bundles of hashish cigarettes. I saw other drugs taken quite openly, swallowed or sniffed with the casualness of habituation. I had never taken drugs before. When I told Duncan this, he only smiled and offered me whatever I wanted. I began to smoke hashish and, as time passed, to experiment with the various pills and powders that people handed me.

For the most part, once the introductions had been dispensed with, Duncan's friends ignored me. I did not belong to their world. I was a brazen intruder, untried, uncouth, with nothing of interest to offer them. Duncan, though on the whole their junior, was at ease among them, and was, indeed, treated with a large measure of respect, though I could not tell on what this might be based.

My days were spent, as in Rabat, studying spoken Arabic with a young student, a timid young man with sleek hair and brown eyes named Mohammed. He was studying law at the Université

Mohammed V, and knew less English than I did French. Our conversations were severely limited. I tried to discover what he knew about my host, but he was either well enough paid or sufficiently frightened to say nothing.

While I struggled with my Arabic or the latest text that had been set for me to read, Duncan was busy visiting friends in town or at one of the small villages along the coast. He never took me with him, though he did try to make up for his absences with extra time spent reading together or just sitting in a local café, talking about his family or mine. After a couple of weeks like this, I began to grow frustrated and angry with him.

"What was the point of bringing me here?" I asked one day when we were alone in the house together. "I don't do anything here that I couldn't do just as easily in Edinburgh. It's stupid, it's just a waste of time."

"Don't call it that," he said. "I never waste time, least of all my own."

"It isn't your time I'm talking about. You do what you want to, see whom you want to see. All I do is sit here and read, or practice verbs with Mohammed."

"I told you when we started: you are here to observe and to listen."

"Observe what?" I asked. "Listen to what? Old men grunting at one another? Old women sniffing cocaine?"

"If I told you in advance, you would see and hear nothing. You must use your own eyes and ears."

"On what? All I ever meet are the old people who come here every night. They don't even speak to me. They couldn't care less about me."

He smiled and shook his head.

"On the contrary," he said, "they care about you very much. And don't you think they are worth observing, worth listening to?"

"When we came here, you said you spent your summers with holy men, men with access to ancient wisdom. I didn't expect to waste my time with a bunch of dried-up old socialites reminiscing about Barbara Hutton and her parties."

His face grew suddenly serious.

"Take care what you say," he warned me. "Take great care. And never say such a thing in front of any of them. Since you are new to such matters, you can be forgiven. But watch and listen with great attention. Some of them *are* holy people, even if they do not seem it. They have wisdom you can only dream of. Not all of them, to be sure—but it is for you to see who has mastery and who has not."

I said nothing more after that, but I started to watch Villiers and his guests more closely. The more I observed, the more I grew aware of gradations of difference between them. Some seemed to be peripheral to whatever was really going on, others to be part of an inner circle whose secrets were privy only to one another. Before long, I noticed that the center of this circle was not, as I might at first have thought, Villiers himself, but a Frenchman, introduced to me as the comte d'Hervilly. I now began to watch the count more closely than the others, to listen when he was talking. Generally, he spoke in French, distinctly enough to allow me to grasp part of what he said.

He was a man in his late sixties, yet by no means weakened with age. Well dressed and elegant almost to the point of affectation, he nevertheless seemed unaware or uncaring of his own physical refinement. I never saw him wear the same suit of clothes twice, yet the changes he made in cut or color were never anything but subtle. He would wear a flower in his buttonhole, a white or a red rose, and it would stay fresh from the beginning to the end of a long, sultry evening.

One evening, on the point of making his departure, he came across to me and asked me to join him for lunch on the following day.

"You have been much neglected," he said. "It is time we remedied that. Come to me at one o'clock. Duncan will tell you where to find my house. But be sure to come alone."

LATER THAT NIGHT, I heard what I took to be feet just outside my room. Thinking it might be Duncan, I went to the door and opened it. There was no one on the landing, but I thought I heard someone creeping away toward the stairs. Duncan had mentioned that there were burglars working in the medina, that residents were taking greater care than usual. I slipped out after the intruder.

When I reached the turn of the corridor, I was able to see through a latticed window straight onto the courtyard below, round which the house was

built. The moon was almost directly overhead, its
light slick on the little fish pond in the center of the
sahn. I looked down, knowing this to be the only
way out of the house. After the darkness in my
room, the light was almost dazzling. It fell
crookedly across a floor of wet tiles, blue and white
rectangles laid in an intricate geometric pattern that
seemed to move. As I watched, I saw a figure
emerge from the house door. It was dressed in a
dark-colored jellaba, black or dark brown, with the
wide hood drawn up over its head.

I opened my mouth to shout, to challenge the
figure below, but my throat was dry and words
would not come. For some reason, I felt terribly
afraid. I continued standing there, my lips open, my
tongue wooden, watching as the hooded figure
stopped, then turned and looked upward in my
direction. If it had a face, it was locked in deep
shadow. I ducked aside, hiding behind the wall for
several heartbeats. When I summoned the courage
to look again, the courtyard was empty. A fish
moved in the pool and grew still. The wet tiles lay
cold in the moonlight. There was no sign that feet
had passed across them moments earlier.

Chapter 10

I SAID NOTHING THE NEXT MORNING about the supposed intruder, and no one said a word over breakfast about a burglary. I knew next to nothing about Villiers and his household: furtive as the hooded man's behavior had seemed, he may very well have been involved in some business that Villiers would prefer to have kept quiet.

After my morning lesson with Mohammed, I headed on foot for the exclusive Marshan quarter on its hill overlooking the sea. D'Hervilly's villa was set behind tall white walls heavy with scented jasmine. A green gate opened to reveal a stepped courtyard, pools, and trees. I was led through cool shuttered rooms to a roof terrace covered in potted flowers and shrubs. D'Hervilly was seated at a table laid for lunch. Glass and silver caught the high

Mediterranean light. My host was dressed in white, and his silver hair seemed part of the setting. Beyond him, I could see the city tumbling chaotically to the harbor, and the blue sea behind, flecked with gold and studded with red- and white-sailed boats.

"Sit down, Mr. Macleod. Please make yourself at home. I am glad to have this opportunity to talk with you alone. Take off that wretched hat, the umbrella will give us more than enough shade."

We dined on bream fresh from the harbor, washed down with a bottle of Oustalet, the best of the local white wines. The sweet was a mint soufflé, and there were chocolates from Debauve & Gallais. D'Hervilly said that his cook was reputed the finest in Tangier, and that the king had once tried to steal him from him. He was not boasting, it was a mere statement of fact, as normal to him as being able to read or write.

We sat afterward in a shaded room hung with carpets, drinking coffee.

"This house is built on the most ancient site in Tangier," D'Hervilly said.

"Roman?" I asked.

He shook his head.

"No, before that before the Carthaginians, before the Phoenicians. It may be as old as the second millennium B.C. The first inhabitants of Tangier built a temple here. There are still some remains—I will show them to you before you leave. But you must promise to speak of it to no one. Its existence has only ever been revealed to a few people. The archaeologists would go crazy if they knew of it;

there would be compulsory purchase orders, God knows what. I would certainly lose this house."

"Is that why you bought it? To have the temple."

He nodded once.

"Of course. Houses are very ordinary things, even ones as beautiful as this. But such temples are a rarity. They are an opportunity to touch the past, to come face to face with ancient wisdom, not as we would like it to have been, but as it truly was. Duncan tells me you have spent time with the Fraternity of the Old Path. What do you think of them? You may be frank with me."

I told him what I thought, and he listened, smiling, but without condescension.

"Yes," he said when I came to an end. "You are perfectly right. They understand the need for ancient wisdom, but they do not know how to come by it. And if they found real knowledge, they would have no idea what to do with it. You are extremely fortunate to have met Duncan. He is not like them, he belongs in a different league entirely. I hope you understand that."

"Yes, I do," I said, meaning it. "I owe everything to him."

"By the time he has finished, you will owe him much more than you can possibly imagine. I knew his father. And my father and his grandfather were close friends. Did he tell you that?"

I shook me head. Three generations, on one side at least. It was quite remarkable.

"He tells me many things," d'Hervilly continued. "For example, he says that you are unhappy here."

I shifted in my chair, embarrassed, not knowing what exactly Duncan had told him. I repeated a little of what I had said to Duncan, somewhat watered down.

"You are not entirely wrong. Some of Villiers's friends are quite superficial. But we endure them for reasons you could not yet understand. Nonetheless, I advise you to stay with Duncan at all costs. His journey here has just begun. You will be changed by the time it finishes. I assure you. I know he has great plans for you. Very great plans."

We talked after that of what I had read and what I planned still to read, and to Duncan's advice d'Hervilly added some suggestions of his own. He had spent time with Jewish rabbis in nearby Chechaouèn, a Rifian town some one hundred kilometers southeast of Tangier. The Jews there—now all vanished, mostly to Israel—had been the descendants of refugees from the Spanish Inquisition and spoke an early form of Castilian long extinct in Spain itself. From them, d'Hervilly had acquired information long thought lost, the key to innumerable Kabbalistic texts.

"When you are ready," he said, "Duncan will send you back to me. I shall introduce you to matters of which even he is ignorant. It will not be next year, it may not be for another ten. But rest assured that the time will come. Now," he said, glancing at a small clock near the door, "let me show you our little temple."

IT WAS NO MORE THAN A TINY, low-ceilinged chamber, cut from solid rock, and located beneath the floor of d'Hervilly's cellar. Although the house itself was cool, the moment I stepped down the ladder into the temple, I felt as if a very ancient and inhuman cold had entered me.

D'Hervilly switched on an overhead lamp that shed a cheerless yellow light on the bare rock. The cold seemed to deepen, to penetrate more sharply beneath the skin. On one wall a tall figure had been carved in the rock, a ram bearing a solar disc between its horns. At its feet, a man stood over the prostrate figure of a victim. On the floor, directly underneath the carving stood a rough block of stone, perhaps a piece of the same rock that had been quarried to create the temple.

As I stood there shivering, I felt wave after wave of depression pass over me. I remembered Catriona's death as though it has just been yesterday. As time passed, the little room filled with other, darker sensations, ugly and uncompromising, as though, in the deepest antiquity, fear and loathing and brutality had been laid down there for all time. Then, underneath all that, I became aware of another sensation, a conviction that I was in the presence of something wholly evil, something darker and older than the earth itself.

I turned to see d'Hervilly watching me intently.

"You feel it?" he asked.

"It's . . . horrible," I said. I felt as though I wanted to be sick.

"Come back upstairs," he said. "You are not ready for this yet."

Back in the cellar, d'Hervilly shut the trapdoor that led to the temple.

"You will return here," he said. "When you are stronger, when you understand more. What you experienced today were the feelings of the victims who died here. The chamber is full of their pain, and if that is what you are attuned to, that is what you will experience. But in time you will see that there are other sensations, and when you are old enough and wise enough, you will be able to share them as well. Feelings of mastery, feelings of deep joy."

We went upstairs to a room overlooking the sea.

"What did you feel exactly?" asked d'Hervilly. "It is best to explain, to bring it into the light."

I told him what I could, finding it hard to put what I had felt into words, however simple.

"The worst thing was the very beginning," I said. "I remember someone I once knew, someone who's dead, and it was as if I were reliving her death. It was as fresh as if it had happened yesterday."

"That is not uncommon," he said. "The room seeks out our griefs and uses them to construct its own sensations in our minds. The first step in overpowering it is to gain control over our own feelings." He paused. "The person you told me about was Catriona, is that right?"

"Yes. How did you know?"

"Duncan told me about her, about how badly her death affected you. I am very sorry. Duncan says she was very beautiful."

"Yes," I said. "And very kind, and very funny. I miss her very much."

"That is natural. Do you have a photograph of her?"

I took one from my pocket and passed it to him. As he took it he smiled. I saw his finger move in the same circular motion that had been described by Duncan's, as though encircling Catriona's face; and he too whispered something inaudible beneath his breath.

"Is this the only one you have?" he asked.

I shook my head.

"No, I have several. I look at them very seldom. But I like to have some with me."

"May I keep this? To help me remember your grief."

I hesitated. I had given the photograph of Catriona's grave freely to Duncan, since I considered him a friend. But d'Hervilly was a comparative stranger. On the other hand, he had just entertained me lavishly and spoken of further visits. He would not be a man to cross lightly.

"Very well," I said. "If you would like it."

"I would like it very much. Duncan was not mistaken. She was beautiful. At my age it is good to be reminded of beauty."

I LEFT HIM SHORTLY AFTER THAT, walking back toward the medina in light that was losing its earlier strength. The air was still warm, but I could feel a freshness in the wind coming from the sea. I was too confused and full of thoughts to want to go straight back to Villiers. Instead, I headed into town, wandering past shops and cafés in the hope of distraction. At the end of boulevard Pasteur, I saw a sign for the main post office, and this reminded me that I had told the secretary of the department back in Edinburgh that, should they need to get in touch with me, I might be contacted at the poste restante in Tangier.

I had a long wait in a queue that seemed frozen by the malign magic of Moroccan bureaucratic inertia. In the end, after many spellings and respellings of my name, I was handed a small pack of letters. There were two from the university, with forms I had to sign, one from New College, saying my services would not be required for the seminar course beginning in the autumn, and one from Harriet Gillespie.

There was a bar a few doors away on Mohammed V. When I had ordered a pastis, I sat down to read Harriet's letter. It was written in a small, hurried hand, the letters well spaced, but somehow carelessly set down, as though time or anxiety pressed her to write without her usual attentiveness.

Iain is ill, she wrote. *He's asked me to write to you, though it isn't easy. Our last meeting wasn't very happy, was it? Maybe the next will be better. But I don't know, I don't know if we should meet again. And I think, I fear Iain may be dying.*

He fell ill a few days after visiting you. It was nothing at first, just a cold that wouldn't leave him. Some weeks after that, he had a fever that lasted for over ten days. He recovered and went back to work, but early in June he grew frettish and his behavior changed. He was cold toward me, something he'd never been. The illness returned, worse than before, with frequent headaches.

The doctors say they don't understand what's wrong. Iain's symptoms don't correspond to anything they're familiar with, their tests show nothing conclusive, their drugs have no effect. He's been in and out of hospital several times now, with no result.

Sometimes the fever passes and he's clear-headed for a day or two. Then the headaches start again, and he has hallucinations. They're very like the ones you told us about, the ones you had last year. Last night, he told me he saw a hooded man in his dreams, in a long, dark street with many voices. Does that mean anything to you?

He wants you to see him. I've told him you're abroad, that you aren't expected back until the end of the summer, and that you may not be contactable; but he insists I try to reach you. There's something he wants to tell you, he won't say what it is. I think he's afraid for you, I think there's something he knows about Mylne.

Andrew, I don't want Iain excited, and I think seeing you would disturb him; but he gets anxious and frets terribly if I try to put off writing. So here's the letter, if it ever reaches you. Come if you can, and if you can't, write. A letter from you might help settle his mind. If you've broken with Mylne, please tell him so, for I think that's who he fears above all else. No, that's not quite right. There's someone else, an associate of Mylne's, someone Iain wants to warn you about. He says there are things you have to know before it's too late.

She had started to write something else here, but had scratched it out and begun over again, perhaps after a little time had passed. Her handwriting was shakier than before.

> *Last night there was something waiting at the foot of the stairs. I don't know what it was or when it will come again. But all the time it waited, Iain's fever was high, and when he regained consciousness he asked if it was still there. I didn't see it, but I heard it.*
>
> *Come if you can, but be quick about it. He's growing weaker every day. I think he cannot have long to last if you do not come and reassure him that all is well.*

> *Harriet*

Chapter

11

WE SET OFF FOR FEZ the following morning. I had come too far to turn back now; and, frankly, I was afraid of what Duncan might do were I to tell him that, instead of continuing with him as arranged, I had to rush to a friend's bedside. I reasoned with myself that Harriet must be exaggerating, that Iain could not be that ill, that Edinburgh had some of the best medical facilities in Europe, that there was plenty of time. The best thing would be to write or phone once I got to Fez.

We arrived by train in the early afternoon, in a different sunshine, beneath another sky. The sea was far behind us now, we were on the foothills of the Middle Atlas, and already my heart was beating differently. I could sense that we had left Europe behind us completely now, even those last remnants that lingered on the streets of Tangier and Casablanca. This was another world entirely, and another century—or, rather, a place where time no longer had any meaning.

Fez, like so many modern cities in North Africa, is divided into two main sections: the old city, or medina, to the north, and the French-built Ville Nouvelle to the southwest. They are separated by more than geography. One is a world of hotels, cafés, and drably smart shops, flat, ordinary, and squalid in its way; the other is darkness and light, a sprawling, dreaming maze of shops and mosques and houses, where the past is everything. And all around, the hills with their vast graveyards rise above the green roofs and the square minarets.

A car was waiting to take us to the old city, a short drive away. We halted in an open area outside the Boujeloud Gate; the driver said we would have to get out there, for cars could not hope to negotiate the alleys of the medina itself.

Something strange happened as we waited for the driver to stack our bags on the ground. Taking us for tourists, a rabble of children and young men surrounded us, offering to act as guides. Duncan said nothing, and I followed his example. Moments later, the shouting voices fell silent. A young man dressed in a white jellaba had appeared by our side and taken Duncan's hand.

The would-be guides fell away like flies, drifting back into the crowd from which they had come. A few continued to watch us from a safe distance, eyeing us with what seemed a mixture of awe and contempt. It was as if word had gone out that we were not to be approached. I saw other tourists, surrounded by small gaggles of tormentors who would not be put off so easily, while we walked like old inhabitants through the gate and into the old city. Behind us, our bags were being strapped on a mule, ready to negotiate the steep, winding lanes between the gate and our destination.

It was the city of my nightmares, that much I knew at once. Tall, windowless buildings crowded in from every side, at every corner, dark, forbidding doorways marked the entrances to a hidden life carried on behind high walls. We soon turned off the thoroughfare of the Talaa Saghira into a maze of progressively narrower and darker alleyways. From time to time, we would pass the open doors of mosques and madrasahs, catching tantalizing glimpses of tiles and bands of swirling calligraphy. A veiled woman would come out and hurry past us, a trader leading a heavily packed mule would shout out "*Balak, balak*," warning us to cram ourselves into the nearest doorway while he passed, a gang of children would fall silent and break off from kicking a ball in order to watch us go by.

The city folded its withered arms about us, very dark and very old, its walls crumbling, its paving stones cracked and misplaced, its noises and smells unutterably alien to me. Alien, yet in a horrible sense, deeply familiar. I kept close to Duncan, who walked along nonchalantly, like someone who has returned to a place he knows well.

The old city is shaped like an elongated basin, sloping inward from the edges toward the center, where the Kairouyine Mosque lies, hidden behind high walls. Our steps were always downward, taking us deeper and deeper toward the city's ancient heart. At last we came to a plain doorway at the end of a *derb*, one of the innumerable short culs-de-sac that branch off the main alleys. I do not think it had a name or needed one. Our guide knocked at the heavy door, and moments later it was opened and we were led inside. A short, unlit passageway led into the sudden sunlight of a tiled courtyard, its stuccoed walls blackened with age, its intricately carved archways faded and crumbling in places. Passing through a second doorway, we entered another courtyard, larger and more gracious than the first, yet in an even greater state of disrepair. Ivy hung from the high wooden latticework, weeds pushed aside the tiles about the central fountain.

I later learned that the house had been in the same family as far back as the twelfth century, since when it had undergone numerous changes. In the fifteenth century it had served as a palace for a succession of governors, in the sixteenth century it had been the home of the celebrated *qadi*, Bu Slimane ibn Yacoub al-Fasi, and in the eighteenth it had enjoyed a reputation for sanctity as the *zawiya* of a dervish order. All this I learned later from Duncan, who knew the house's history intimately.

A curtained doorway led to a flight of unlit wooden stairs, at whose top we found a long, wood-paneled room. I could see very little at first. The only light came through the tall latticed windows that looked out onto the courtyard from which we had just come. It lay in puzzling geometrical shapes on all manner of unguessable objects, on faded carpets and brass lamps hanging by long chains from a ceiling lost in shadow, on tall candlesticks and ebony Qur'an stands, on low tables inlaid with ivory writing, on books and reed pens and inkstands.

The young man who had led us here vanished, leaving Duncan and myself alone in this silent room. I felt suddenly afraid. Of the unknown, certainly, for everything familiar had been snatched away from me. Of my own ability to cope with the curious demands now being made on me. Of an irrational voice in my head that trotted out rubbish about the white slave trade and murders of foreigners in North Africa.

But there was more than that, and I knew it, even if I could not articulate it. The room reminded me of d'Hervilly's cold temple, there was an identical sensation of dread seeping through the carpeted walls, the same knowledge that I was in the presence of a very old and very powerful force of evil.

A voice came from the far end of the room, a thin, cold voice that I almost thought I recognized.

"Taqarrabu, ya rufaqa'i." Come close, my friends.

Duncan went ahead of me, confident as ever. He had been here before, he knew what to expect. And whom. I followed a couple of steps behind him, straining to see more clearly in the muted light. Slowly, my eyes were growing used to the dimness.

On a low divan at the head of the room sat an old man. When I say that he was old, you must not think I mean seventy or eighty years old. He was visibly much, much more ancient than that. Later, Duncan told me he thought he might be as much as two hundred years old. I refused to believe it at the time. Now, I am not so sure.

He wore traditional dress, and at first I thought he might almost have been a mummy wrapped in the robes of an eighteenth-century sheikh. Long, desiccated fingers lay like claws on his lap. A thin white beard straggled down toward a narrow chest. The cheeks were hollow, the mouth devoid of teeth. But the eyes were as full of life as any I had ever seen. I flinched as they caught me and held me. They had more strength in them than a young man's hands.

"*Tfeddlu, glesu,*" he said, falling into the colloquial. "Please sit down."

We sat on the carpet in front of him, crossing our legs. He took his eyes from me and looked at Duncan, smiling. It was an ugly, misshapen smile. I looked away, concentrating on a band of light that fell slanting across the wall behind the old man.

"*Vous avez voyagé longtemps pour me rejoindre ici,*" he said, his French stilted, almost as if he had not spoken the language in a long time.

"*Pas de tout,*" responded Duncan. "*Cela me fait grand plaisir de vous revoir. Et de voir que vous êtes toujours en bonne santé.*"

"*U-nta, kif s-shiha?*"

"*La bas.*"

They began to talk rapidly in Moroccan Arabic,

leaving me behind. I could make no sense of what they said, picking up only obvious words in every other sentence. Duncan was clearly in awe of our host, yet at ease with him. Tea was brought by the young man we had met earlier, sweet green tea in silver pots stuffed with fresh mint. The young man poured it into thin glasses and left it with us, sending out clouds of mint-scented steam into the cool air.

Duncan and the old man talked at length, and as they did the light moved across the wall and grew dim. Outside, the sun was dropping, and the city was returning to darkness. I heard my name mentioned more than once, though I could not understand what they said about me. The old man looked at me each time, then away again. I did not return his gaze.

There was a brief silence, then I heard the old man speak again, and I knew that this time he was addressing me.

"*Wa anta, ya Andrew,*" he said, shifting to classical Arabic. "*Limadha hadarta amami? A-anta tajir aw talib?*"

I could not grasp all he said, and turned to Duncan for help.

"He asks why you have appeared before him. He asks if you are a merchant or a seeker."

"I don't understand."

"It is what he once asked my grandfather. Angus Mylne came to Fez to trade in cloth and left a seeker after true knowledge."

"What did your grandfather answer?"

"He does not need you to tell him that. You must give your own answer."

I looked at the old man. His eyes had not once left me.

"*Ana talib al-haqq,*" I answered. "I have come in search of the truth."

"*Mahma kalifa 'l-amr?*"

I did not understand. I looked at Duncan.

"He is asking you 'Will you carry on the search whatever the price?'"

I felt confused.

"You know I have no money, Duncan. I can't afford to—"

Duncan frowned and raised his hand gently, quieting me.

"He does not mean money. Perhaps I did not translate well. Whatever the sacrifice, whatever may be required—that would be nearer the mark."

I felt uneasy. What did the old man want from me? What might he demand in future? I did not even know who he was.

"You must trust him," Duncan said. "You must put yourself in his hands if you are to find what you are looking for."

I turned to face the old man. There was so little flesh on his cheeks, he might have been dead but for the eyes.

"*Na'm,*" I said, "*mahma kalifa.*" Yes, whatever it costs.

He looked at me and smiled. I felt a little sick, watching that little toothless mouth contort itself; but I had come this far, I could not turn back. The next moment, the mouth opened and the old man spoke again, except that the voice was not his voice.

"Is this all there is, Andrew? Please tell me. Tell me there's more than this."

It was Catriona's voice. They were the last words she had ever spoken to me.

Chapter 12

His name was Sheikh Ahmad ibn Abd Allah, and I saw him every morning for the next month. I would sit at his feet while he read to me from the works of the medieval Arab sages and elucidated them for me. His erudition was vast, his insight the result, not of knowledge, but of direct experience. I never lost my fear of him, nor my sense that in some way he meant me great harm.

I put the incident of Catriona's voice down to the strain of travel or the effect of drugs I had been given in Tangier. When I mentioned it to Duncan, he merely said that in the sheikh's house a man might see or hear whatever was in his heart. At the time, it seemed a reasonable explanation, and one that it suited me to believe, for to have thought it anything but a self-generated hallucination might well have sent me over the edge of madness. I was wholly uprooted from all that had been familiar to me, alone and effectively stranded in a strange city that seemed to belong to another century. In consequence, I found myself turning more than ever to Duncan as the one stable point in a world without fixed referents.

He told me a little of the sheikh, explaining that he had been responsible for introducing his grandfather to the inner world of Arab occultism.

"I can scarcely believe it possible," I said. "Unless your grandfather was very old at the time, and the sheikh very young."

"This was in 1898, when my grandfather was fifty-two, about the same age I am now. In the account he left of their meeting, he wrote that the sheikh was already an old man then. My grandfather spent seven years studying with Sheikh Ahmad. I have photographs of them together: you can see them when we get back to Edinburgh. The sheikh is younger in the photographs than he is now; but he still seems about eighty or ninety."

"And you're sure it is the same man?"

Duncan looked hard at me.

"I have been coming here for most of my adult life. There is very little I would not believe."

WHEN I WAS NOT WITH THE SHEIKH or Duncan, I was permitted to make use of the library. This was a vast, disorganized room on the first floor, to the north of the chamber in which the sheikh lived. It was filled from floor to ceiling with printed and manuscript texts in Arabic, Hebrew, Turkish, Persian, Greek, and Latin. There was nothing on the shelves that dated from later than the eighteenth century. Time, it seemed, had truly stood still here.

It was wearying work, for the texts I was set to read were frequently stultifying, and the library, though full of shadows, remained hot for much of the day. I began to spend long hours at its latticed windows, gazing out onto a courtyard that was visited by small birds and at certain hours dappled with sunshine. It served to remind me that another world still existed outside this, that I had not been swallowed entirely by the darkness.

At the end of the first week, I asked if I were to be confined to the house, or whether I might not profit by seeing the city for myself. Duncan told me I should not be foolish, I was of course free to go where I liked and when I pleased, provided I could be sure to return to Sheikh Ahmad's house before it grew dark.

And so I began to explore the lanes and alleyways of old Fez, mapless, guideless, with only my own wits to lead me through the maze. I became a sort of ghost, treading almost unseen down long, murky corridors of mud and cobble between blank walls, glimpsing what I could of a world that had changed little or not at all in centuries.

I saw other Europeans, Americans, Australians, small parties of Japanese, all huddled together, twittering like birds of passage on this latest stage of their travels, bright, careless people for whom Fez was merely a stage set erected for their amusement.

I never tried to join any of them, never attempted to engage them in conversation, never so much as thought to leave with one of their parties and return home. I was by now wholly remote from whatever I had once been, I had been drawn deeply into realms no rational mind could encompass.

Each day the city revealed a little more of itself to me, at the same time shutting something else away or making clear that it had secrets to which I might never penetrate. I watched tanners and dyers go about their work, stood for hours watching metalworkers hammer trays, sat with carpenters as they turned cedarwood for beds and chairs and tables. At the butchers' shops, flies lay like a seething film on the flanks of meat. Patches of damp appeared on the sides of buildings, like sweat. Open sewers lay unattended, filling the air with their stench. I walked for hours each day, lost among sounds and sights and smells I could only partially understand. And in the late afternoon, wherever I was, I would turn back to the sheikh's house, hurrying through the lengthening shadows, pursued by my own echoing footsteps.

One day, when we had been about three weeks in Fez, I entered a stationer's shop in order to buy a fresh notebook and a few pens. When I say "shop," I mean one of those tiny one-room emporia that form the basis of every souk, raised up about three feet above the ground. As I was paying for my goods, I noticed that there was a telephone on the wall at the back, and I remembered my plan to ring Harriet in order to ask about Iain.

Edinburgh seemed such a long way away, and

Iain and Harriet more like characters from a book than flesh-and-blood friends whom I had last seen not many months earlier. All the same, I felt terribly guilty about having let things slip for so long, and offered the owner of the shop enough money to enable me to make a call to Britain. Impressed by my use of Arabic, he readily agreed.

I rang Iain and Harriet's number and felt a wave of homesickness when the familiar ringing tone began. The phone rang for over a minute before anyone answered. An unfamiliar voice came on the line, a woman's voice, plain and non-committal.

"Gillespie."

"Is Harriet there?" I asked.

"No, Harriet's away. She's not in Edinburgh."

"I need to speak to her. Do you know where I can reach her?"

"She can't be reached. Who is this?"

"I'm a friend. I'm ringing to see how Iain is. I had a letter from Harriet saying he was ill."

There was a pause. I could hear the line crackling as though we were about to be cut off.

"Iain is dead," the woman answered. I could sense an emotion in her voice, quickly suppressed. "He died in hospital four weeks ago. I'm very sorry if . . . "

I put the phone down. My hand was shaking. The stationer asked if I was all right. I nodded briskly and made my escape, leaving my notebook and pens behind.

Once or twice, looking over my shoulder as I stumbled back to the sheikh's house, I thought I caught a glimpse of someone walking behind me. A man in a dark jellaba, as though dressed for winter, with the hood pulled up high over his head.

I DID NOT SLEEP THAT NIGHT. Iain had urgently wanted to see me, and I had let him down. He had died without speaking to me, and somehow this made me feel guilty, as though I had been in some way responsible for his death. I tried for several hours to compose a letter to Harriet, but each time I tore up my attempt, until I finally accepted that anything I said would only make things worse. Perhaps I could visit her when I returned to Edinburgh.

Somewhere across the city, a wedding was in progress. The festivities would continue into the early hours of the morning, even after the groom had been taken to his bride and her bloodstained undergarments produced for friends and relatives to see as evidence of her virginity. Loudspeakers droned out a mixture of traditional music and *rai*, and from time to time the voices of guests would be carried on the night air, raucous and excited.

Around three o'clock, the music fell silent and the city was returned to peace. In an hour or so, the muezzins would chant the call to the *fajr* prayer. The day would begin. But now there was silence throughout the city once more, and it was still the middle of the night.

I found it impossible to remain in my room. After the music, the silence and darkness seemed insupportable. I rose and left my room, heading downstairs to the library courtyard, where I could sit and watch until the first signs of dawn touched the sky. The house was like a tomb. Nothing stirred. I crossed the landing and reached the top of the stairs, just opposite the entrance to the sheikh's room. As I made to pass it, I noticed that the door was open and that a faint light was just visible inside.

I do not know why I stopped, nor what made me step inside the room. My eyes had grown so accustomed to the darkness that my surroundings appeared well lit even though only a couple of oil lamps were burning. The room seemed to draw me in, as though in some sense possessed of a life and a magnetism of its own. I stepped forward hesitantly, straining to see ahead.

The silence was absolute, forbidding. I knew I was intruding, yet I felt I could not turn back. I wanted to see what this room was like while the sheikh was sleeping. As I drew closer to the far end I could see the outline of the old man's divan. This was where I normally sat in the mornings to read with him. There would be soft sunlight on the cushions and blankets on which he sat, and on the carpeted floor. Now shadows surrounded everything.

A single lamp was lit near one end of the long divan. There was something strange about the upper half of the divan, as though bedding or laundry had been left on it. I stepped a little closer, and as I did so realized that the sheikh himself was lying there, flat on his back, dressed in a long white garment. It should have occurred to me before that he must sleep here, and not in another room as I had supposed.

I should have left the room then, but I did not. Something about the figure on the divan held my attention. He was very still, more like a reclining statue than a man asleep. The longer I stood, the more curious his stillness seemed to me. At last, I summoned up enough courage to walk forward until I was only a foot or two away.

I looked down at him. A minute passed, then another. He did not move. His chest did not rise or fall, no breath passed his lips. There could be no question: the old man had died and was lying here until they came for him in the morning. I started to reach out a hand to touch his cheek, as though by doing so I could be certain that he was dead. As I did so, a voice spoke behind me, in a whisper.

"Go back to your room, Andrew. You should not have come here. This is nothing for you to meddle with."

I spun round. Duncan was standing behind me. Like the sheikh, he was dressed from head to foot in white. He did not seem like the man I had travelled so far with, the man I had known back home in Edinburgh.

I opened my mouth, eager to explain, to apologize, but he silenced me.

"Leave now," he said. "Quickly. I cannot be responsible if you stay."

There was a note of fear in his voice that chimed perfectly with what I felt inside, with what the silence and the shadows and the still figure on the divan were already shouting at me. I ran from the room and did not stop until I was in my own room, shaking and praying for dawn.

Chapter

13

I MUST HAVE FALLEN ASLEEP. A hand on my shoulder woke me, causing me to jump. It was Duncan, come for me at the usual time.

"The sheikh is expecting you, Andrew. You should not be late."

I looked at him, not understanding.

"The sheikh? But—"

Duncan put his fingers to his lips and shook his head gently.

"Say nothing of what you saw last night. I will explain it all to you in time. But for the moment, you must behave as though you know nothing. It is for the best."

I dressed and breakfasted on black coffee, as had become my custom in that house, and when it was time, I made my way to the sheikh's room.

He was waiting for me as always, a stiff figure held erect more by willpower than muscle, his thin legs crossed beneath his robes, his head balanced on his neck like a shell on a wooden stalk. On his lap lay a sheet of white paper covered by his long, bird-like hands. I had never felt so afraid of anyone before.

"You look tired," were his first words after I had greeted him and seated myself on the floor at his feet.

"There was a wedding last night," I said. "The music kept me awake."

He stared past me into the room.

"They marry," he murmured, "they give birth, they die. I have heard the music of more weddings in this city than you can possibly imagine. And the weeping of funeral processions just as often."

His eyes turned to me.

"What would you give to escape all that?" he asked. "Marriage, birth, decay, the grave."

I hesitated. Every word mattered here, there could be no carelessness.

"Surely," I stammered, "surely no one can escape the grave."

He looked hard at me without answering. I felt the slow heartbeat in my chest quicken its tempo. This was dangerous territory. A word or phrase out of place . . .

"On the contrary," he said, "that has been the object of our brief study here. The means of escape."

"In theory, yes, I understand that. But . . . surely no one could really achieve it." As I spoke, however, I thought of what I had witnessed the night before. Had Sheikh Ahmad cheated the grave? Had he really been an old man one hundred years earlier? And a century before that?

"You are very young," he said, "and your studies of these matters have scarcely begun. Do not leap to conclusions. In time you will understand."

He paused. His withered hands moved like leaves across his lap, disturbing the sheet of paper.

"You have not yet answered my question," he said. "What would you give to live even one year beyond your allotted span?"

"I have no desire to live a long life," I replied. "There would be no point in it."

"Really? Why is that?"

"Because the point of everything for me was someone I loved. She died, and I can no longer see a point to anything."

"I understand. You said it when you first came, that you do not seek longevity but mastery. But what if I were to say to you that this woman whom you loved might be brought back to life again?"

He did not take his eyes off me as he said it.

"That would be very cruel," I said. "Catriona is dead. Her body is in a grave, rotting."

"Nevertheless." His voice was hard, unyielding. "If it were said. What would you give? I ask you merely to suppose."

"To have her back?" I thought it safest to play his game. "Everything," I said. "I would give everything."

"Your own life? Your soul?"

"Yes," I said. "If it would bring her back. Anything at all."

He smiled for the first time.

"You have started to learn," he said.

He lifted his hands from his lap. The paper that lay on his knee had inscribed on it a circular talisman of the style known in Arabic as *da'ira*. In the center, prominent among a host of invocations, I could see Catriona's name, written in red ink in Arabic characters.

WE LEFT FEZ THE FOLLOWING DAY. Of what followed I retain but the haziest memory. Our first destination was Marrakesh, where we took a small house of our own in the medina, and where Duncan was visited daily by a succession of holy men and seers. This far south, the summer heat was oppressive. The long days passed in a sort of narcoleptic state in which I was more asleep than awake. I longed for a cool breeze or an ice-filled stream. Everything wilted. My dreams were filled with memories of Sheikh Ahmad. His withered face and feverish eyes harried me down long, dusty streets. Sometimes he was dead, sometimes alive, sometimes something that was neither the one thing nor the other. Several times I dreamed that Iain and Catriona were looking for me and could not find me.

Duncan grew morose and withdrawn, his bonhomie worn down by the constant heat and the long hours he sat incarcerated with his holy men, reciting spells or reading grimoires their fathers had passed down to them. He would introduce me to those of them he thought it suitable for me to meet. And we went together at night to visit the ceremonies of their brotherhoods or to recite prayers at the tombs of their sheikhs.

From Marrakesh we traveled into the deep south, to the Tafilalt and beyond. The few towns through which we passed were stranger than any dream, labyrinthine warrens built to shut out the desert sun. Here I would sit for hours in darkness while Duncan whispered in the corner with men in veils and old women tattooed with henna on their hands and feet. I would fall asleep only to find myself crawling through the door of that dark cathedral in Stornoway or hurrying on all fours down the streets of Fez, pursued by something that slithered and sang.

We passed through an unchanging waste of desert in which the tiny huddled towns were mere growths of sand-colored brick, the monotony broken only by the occasional white dome of a saint's *koubba* or a human figure etched against the skyline. Everywhere we went, they spoke of the dead, the *amwat*. They wore amulets to guard against unseen evil, they carried talismans to ward off the attentions of the undead. In cemeteries set hard against the desert, they would whisper to us the secrets of the next world. I shivered, thinking of the old man in Fez, for I knew he had been dead that night.

One day toward the end of September, Duncan told me it was time to return home.

"We're finished here for this year," he said. "I know it hasn't been easy for you, but when you get back and sort it all out, you'll see how valuable it's been. You've learned more in these few months than you could have learned in years at home."

We journeyed back to Marrakesh, where we were to take a plane back to London. Duncan had booked us into a hotel and allowed two days in which to rest before the flight. We were both tired and in need of sleep, and much of the time was spent in bed.

On the last evening, we returned to the hotel after an early meal. We both had some packing to do. The streets were filled with people heading for the *moussem* of Sidi Musa, a local saint, a festival that would continue for several days. The sound of music floated across the roofs. In a small square next to our hotel, men were preparing to slaughter sheep in honor of the holy man. Some had been despatched already. There was a tang of blood on the air. The night was hot, but with a touch of damp that heralded the coming rains.

Indoors, we went to our rooms to finish packing. I had about a dozen books that had been given to me in the course of the journey, and I found that the last five would not fit into the suitcase I had planned to fly back with. Taking them with me, I went to Duncan's room.

He was standing by an open window, watching the celebrants pass along the street. I could hear the frightened voices of sheep mingling with the shouts of the passersby.

"I can't get all my books in," I said. "Should I try to find another bag?"

"The shops are all closed," he answered. He did not turn from the window. "But there's still some room in my case. You'll find it in the bedroom. Do what you can with them."

I thanked him and went into the bedroom. Duncan's case was lying open on the bed; he had left a few shirts ready to place on top. I lifted a few items out in order to make room for the books. They fitted with room to spare.

As I made to straighten the clothes, something drew my attention. I do not know why. Perhaps I had unconsciously been looking for it. A length of striped cloth, quite unmistakable. A New College scarf—Iain's scarf, the one he had left in my flat, the one that had disappeared shortly after Duncan's arrival. I pulled it out. There was no mistake: Iain's name was written quite clearly on the label. I remembered the conversation I had once had with Duncan about good and evil, and his remark concerning the method by which one might cause a man to fall ill or die. *The most that is needed is a lock of the victim's hair or an article of his clothing to be his representative.*

I returned the scarf carefully to the place it had occupied, tidied the clothes, and left the case as it had been. I went back to Duncan's living room. He was still standing at the window.

Outside, they were slaughtering sheep. I heard them bleating as they were led to the knife. Bleating and stamping their feet on the hard ground. It was the longest night of my life.

Chapter 14

I GOT BACK TO EDINBURGH as the year turned. The leaves had fallen early, and by the middle of October autumn was showing the first signs of hardening into winter. After that interminable summer, I came without warning into a cold and unwelcoming world full of sharp winds, and rain, and mists from the sea. Everywhere I went, people were wrapped against the foul weather. My old rooms were still waiting for me, and I sat in them shivering, loath to go outside.

The summer had unsettled and confused me, bringing with its fresh knowledge a swarm of unanswered questions. My discovery of Iain's scarf in Duncan's luggage had awakened the darkest suspicions, but I felt powerless to pursue them, even in the safety of my own mind. I convinced myself that there must be an innocent explanation, that Duncan had mistaken the scarf for one of his own of similar design. College scarves are easily confused for one another. But I also knew what use could be made of a scrap of clothing by a man like Duncan.

My job at the university had been irrevocably terminated; there was no immediate prospect of part-time work there or at Herriot-Watt, the city's other university, so I signed on for unemployment benefit. I would be worse off, but I reasoned that I would gain by having the freedom to spend my days as I pleased and to channel my research in the directions I wanted.

I explained my situation to Duncan as best I could, without revealing the true circumstances. I had completed my doctorate, I said, but wanted to stay in Edinburgh if possible in order to pursue what I now regarded as my real studies. He did not ask when the degree ceremony was to be held, and I think he had guessed the truth by then but decided to go along with my little subterfuge. To be honest, I was tempted to make a clean breast of things: it hardly mattered what sort of research I had been doing, since that was no longer the motivation for my continued involvement with Duncan and his activities. Only embarrassment kept me from admitting what I had been up to earlier.

Duncan immediately offered to pay the rent on my flat, for I could no longer afford to stay there on the little money I had from the state. I said I could not possibly accept.

"You've already paid a small fortune to take

me to Morocco and keep me there," I said. "I can't let you spend another penny on me."

"Hardly a fortune, Andrew. Morocco is a cheap place to live, and we were guests in friends' houses most of the time. I'd prefer to help you. Frankly, I've invested a great deal in you and your arcane education. I'm not prepared to let you go just like that. If you end up in some miserable tenement you'll soon start thinking twice and three times about staying on to study with me. You're fully qualified now, and I don't think you'll have much trouble finding a job of some sort. Once you do that, we'll see less and less of one another. You may even find an academic post in another city." He paused. "You can repay me later."

"How can I do that unless I take a job?"

He smiled.

"Don't worry," he said. "I'm sure I'll think of a way."

The smile did not leave his face. It was warm and winning but curiously knowing, not a pleasant smile at all. I still admired Duncan then, in spite of my fear. And what he was offering was unquestionably attractive.

My experiences in Morocco had disturbed me, but paradoxically whetted my appetite for a more comprehensive grasp of the mysteries I had been investigating. Edinburgh, with its familiar streets and raw winds quickly drove all images of the summer out of my mind. Confused as they had already been, my memories of North Africa grew increasingly hazy, and before many weeks had passed I had come to regard much of what had happened to me there as little more than the work of an already unsettled imagination stimulated by new sights and sounds.

I returned to my books and my rituals. Winter settled hard as steel. There was rain most days, and frost when there was not. I woke late and read through the long nights. I had made a prison for myself, a tightly spun cocoon from which I hoped one day to reemerge, resplendent. But whether I would wake into light or darkness it was impossible to say.

EARLY IN NOVEMBER, Duncan took me to his home for the first time. Penshiel House was a somber dwelling in the Scottish baronial style, situated to the east of the city, at the foot of the Lammermuir Hills. It was a cold, bleak day, with a sky that threatened sleet or even snow. As we drew near the house, rolling down a long, twisting drive in Duncan's Jaguar, it seemed to me that the air grew darker still. Penshiel House lay hidden behind a wall of high trees, their branches already leafless. There were shadows everywhere: the shadows of trees, the shadows of tall rocks, the long shadows of the house itself, thrown crookedly across a short lawn lined with cypresses.

I half expected a bent old man to open the door to us, a faithful retainer who had served father and son all his working life. But instead we were welcomed by a well-dressed middle-aged woman who seemed more personal assistant than house-keeper. Her manner was formal and a trifle severe, and I noticed that she seemed torn between sub-servience and familiarity when speaking to Duncan. An old retainer, then, caught out somehow between the style of one era and the next, between service to a crusty father and devotion to a son from whom she had known greater latitude.

We had lunch in a low-ceilinged dining room at a table built to seat at least twenty. The food was served by a girl of about sixteen who shuffled in and out without a word and responded to Duncan's occasional queries in monosyllables or grunts. She did not seem retarded in any way; but watching her serve, I noticed that she kept her distance from Duncan and avoided touching him. She was a pretty girl, and at first I thought there might be something sexual in their relationship.

On reflection, I dismissed the idea as improbable: Duncan had never seemed to me gross or demanding in that way. But I retained an uneasy impression that something else was wrong. The girl seemed watchful of Duncan, as though afraid of him, and not merely as her employer.

I had, to be honest, often wondered about Duncan's private life. When I thought about it, I realized that I had seen no evidence of sexual activ-ity on his part at all. I had long since disabused myself of the idea that he might be in pursuit of me and that the study of magic was merely a sub-terfuge under which to contrive my seduction. For all that, I had no evidence one way or the other as to his precise orientation in such matters.

He might very well be homosexual, afraid of coming out on account of his career. Or maybe he was simply uninterested in sex, as some people are. Certainly, I had never heard him speak even obliquely of a woman with whom he was involved, now or in the past. It had crossed my mind more than once that he might have dedicated himself to a life of denial, the better to achieve the occult powers he sought. Celibacy was not uncommon among devotees of the magical arts, and more than once in my reading I had come across passages advocating renunciation as a means of preserving a man's vital force.

"This is a large house to live in alone," I said. The girl had gone, we were sitting in a small study drinking coffee.

"I'm not entirely alone," replied Duncan. "There's Miss Melrose. Before young Jennie, there was another girl called Colette, a French girl; she left to get married a year ago. I have a cook, Mrs. Dunbar, a man who looks after the house, and a gardener. They all sleep here. It's quite a little household."

"But not a family."

He shook his head.

"No, there's been no family at Penshiel House since my parents died."

A large fire burned in the open grate, painting the walls a deep copper color. Duncan paused and stared at the flames. A pine log shifted, throwing up sparks as it turned, bright like pieces of cold metal.

"I was married once," he said. "Just like you. And like yours, my wife died. Her name was Constance. She lived here with me. We were very happy, happier than I would have thought was possible. Sometimes it seems long ago, and sometimes just a day or two, no more. If Constance were to walk in here now, it would not surprise me."

To my dismay, I saw that his cheeks were wet with tears. It was the first weakness I had seen in him, the first sign of emotion. The knowledge of it made me feel strangely ill at ease, as though it awakened an echoing weakness in myself.

We finished our coffee in silence. The fire died down slowly, restoring our sense of ease. The shadows covered my embarrassment. Duncan, I think, had none; he wept for himself and for his dead wife, as though alone. He looked up at last and smiled.

"I'm growing morbid," he said. "I'm sorry. Let me show you round before it gets dark."

IT WAS A LARGE HOUSE, full of crooked corridors and tricks of perspective. No floor seemed quite level, a section here or a room there would be divided from the rest by a short flight of steps or a low, sloping passage. In keeping with the style of the exterior, there were turrets reached by spiral staircases, and tall mullioned windows that looked out onto the gardens and the dark, encircling trees.

"The house was built for my grandfather by John Chesser," Duncan said. "It was one of his first commissions, before Southfield. William Burn worked on part of the interior, though he was getting on in years by then. It's never been extended: neither my father nor I cared to interfere with the original design."

In truth, the house seemed little altered since the end of the last century. There were a few concessions to modernity: electricity had been installed, there was central heating in the main rooms, the kitchen had a gas cooker, a single telephone dating from the sixties stood in the hall. Otherwise, the furnishings, carpets, curtains, and ornaments belonged to a different age. Even the potted plants seemed to have been preserved.

"I have the feeling," I said, "that, if your grandfather were to come back, he'd find himself at home."

Duncan nodded, glancing round him.

"He'd find little changed, that's true. And the whole world different."

His voice sounded sad, as though he regretted the passing of time and some sort of loss of innocence.

We continued our slow tour of the house. When we had finished, there was still just enough light for a walk in the gardens. It was only then, as we strolled through the grounds, that something else struck me about Penshiel House. I had seen no portraits, no family photographs, nothing to show who had lived and died there. I did not want to reawaken the unhappiness I had seen earlier in Duncan, and so did not mention this curious absence of his ancestors and family. But I thought about it that night and afterward many times.

Toward the end of our walk, it began to snow, lightly at first, then heavily, thick flakes elbowing their way through the freezing air to cover the bare earth. We went inside at once and Duncan ordered tea and scones. The tea was a light Japanese Kokeicha that had come from a shop in Harrogate, and there was homemade shortbread, sweet and buttery and melting. I relaxed again, seduced by the comfort of the surroundings and the wholesomeness of the food. Duncan had recovered his sangfroid and charm, and he regaled me with elaborate stories of Penshiel House and its inhabitants.

Afterward, he led me to the library, which I had not yet seen, and conducted me round its tall bays of densely packed shelves. There were volumes here I had never seen, editions too precious to be brought out of safekeeping here. In shallow niches between the window bays, the busts of Roman and Greek poets watched us. There were deep shadows in every corner, and all along the narrow balustrade that ran along the library's second story. Sometimes I felt a need to turn, as though we were being watched by more than statues. I remembered with an involuntary shudder the library in Ainslie Place, where I had found the copy of the *Matrix Aeternitatis*.

Chapter

15

BY THE TIME WE FINISHED, it had grown late. Jennie brought us a light supper that we ate off trays in the kitchen.

"I'd better get you back before this storm gets any worse," said Duncan, going to fetch our coats. Jennie and Miss Melrose had already gone to bed. I put my coat on and followed him to the door.

The storm had already worsened. It had turned to a blizzard all the time we had been closeted in the library, and was now firmly fastened on the countryside. The drive was thick with snow, and drifts had started to form in places.

"I'll try to get through if you really want me to," said Duncan. "But I think you'll be better off staying the night."

I had little choice. It was not all that far to the

city, and in a good car like Duncan's, I'm sure we could have made it. But the inconvenience of driving in such conditions, not to mention the not inconsiderable risk of getting stuck on the way back were scarcely problems I could in all conscience impose on my host. I nodded agreement, and we went back inside.

Miss Melrose was roused to make up a bed for me. I was to sleep in a comfortable room overlooking a long meadow that sloped up to a copse of tall firs at the rear of the house. A fire was lit, and hot-water bottles made ready to air and warm the bed. It was all quite an adventure, I thought, to be snowbound in the countryside, in a house such as this, with a fire and servants and the prospect of breakfast in the dining room before a bank of blazing logs. I thanked Duncan for his kindness and retired with a copy of Scott's *Bride of Lammermoor*, whose action is set in not far from Penshiel House.

I did not read for long. The fire had warmed the room rapidly to a pleasant temperature, and the bed, with its heavy covers and piping hot bottles presented an irresistible temptation against which the tribulations of the Master of Ravenswood and Lucy Ashton were but a trifling defence. I undressed and snuggled down beneath the bed-clothes. Already drowsy, I switched off the light and was soon heavily asleep.

It must have been about three o'clock when I woke. The wind had fallen, leaving a tangible silence in its wake. Though the fire had died down almost to nothing, the room was still warm and stuffy, and under my quilts and bedclothes I was perspiring freely. The excessive heat must have woken me, or so I reckoned. Or had it been something else, a noise perhaps? I listened carefully, but could hear nothing, whether inside or outside the house. For some reason, my heart was beating more rapidly than usual.

A small battery-operated lamp had been left on my bedside table by Duncan. I switched it on, lighting the room imperfectly. Drawing back the bed linen, I swung my feet to the floor, grateful for the cooler air that brushed my skin. I felt a sudden need to use the bathroom, and desperately tried to remember where it was situated.

Slipping on my trousers and a sweater, I opened the door, bringing the bedside light with me. I remembered that the nearest bathroom was along a short stretch of corridor and down a flight of some six or seven stairs. Duncan had pointed it out to me on the way to the bedroom.

Leaving my door partly open, I headed off along the freezing passage, eager to get it over with and scurry back to my room. It was bitterly cold, and the overpowering heat of a few moments before had already started to seem desirable. I felt vulnerable and ill at ease walking through those silent, shadow-infested corridors in a house I barely knew.

The bathroom was where I had remembered, an old-style affair with stained white porcelain and wooden panels. When I flushed the toilet, the sound seemed to vibrate through the entire house. The cistern refilled slowly. Somewhere out of sight a water pipe banged in the silence.

As I crept back to my room, I wished I had gone back to Edinburgh earlier, while there was still an option. The house was still and brooding, its silences pregnant with a sense of menace and melancholy. Nothing was quite what it seemed. The heavy wallpaper concealed leering faces and prying eyes among its whorls and vortices.

After the uncompromising cold of the passage, my room again felt overheated and stuffy. Leaving my light on the bedside table, I crossed to the window and drew aside the curtain.

Outside, the sky had cleared, leaving a swathe of brilliant stars and a sharply etched moon. All the ground was iced with snow. A silver landscape sloped away from me, ending in a dark, serrated band of trees that almost touched the moon. I had never seen such stillness, or whiteness so intensified. Unclipping the catch, I pushed the window open. It slid up on the sash without a sound, and I leaned forward, breathing in the ice-cold air.

I sat there for a long time, invigorated and entranced. Behind me, the batteries in my lamp slowly died, but I did not break away from the window in order to switch on the main light. The moon traveled in a shallow arc above the trees, immense and trembling, like a nocturnal creature stalking the night sky. I had never known such peace or such silence since leaving Lewis. My assumptions about Penshiel House were manifestly false. There could be no room for evil in a place where such loveliness existed.

I began to grow cold. As I reached up to draw the window down again, something caught my eye.

It might have been there some time, but unnoticed on account of its position a little below the line of the trees, near where the meadow reached them. Reaching for the window, my eye had been brought downward, permitting me to see that part of the landscape more clearly.

I think it was the movement that caught my eye. I held my breath, thinking that I had surprised a fox or a squirrel moving across the snow. But it was larger than a fox or a squirrel, big enough to be a wolf, I thought. Except that there are no wild wolves in Scotland now.

As I watched, the creature moved again, crawling in the direction of the house, down the gently sloping face of the meadow. It had long legs and moved awkwardly, more like a spider or a crab than an animal of the forest accustomed to walk on all fours. As I watched it come toward me, I felt more than simple cold rush through me. There was something unnatural about the thing on the ground, yet it had an almost human quality about it. I could not tear myself from the window, horrified and frightened though I was. The creature moved slowly, yet with determination, across the still surface of the open field, dragging its limbs through the snow, and leaving in its wake a narrow furrow.

From time to time, it would halt and lift its head, as though sniffing the air. Was it hunting? Was it blind and merely questing? As it reached a point about halfway, I could see it more clearly, though mercifully not in any detail. It stopped again and raised its front quarters, then raised its head, and I was sure that long matted hair, like a woman's hair, trailed from it, and that it was in some sense human.

It continued its halting progress toward the house. I had a horror of it now, a mounting loathing that urged me to close the window and huddle beneath my blankets. But it was light outside and dark in my room now, and I could not face the darkness. The thing shuffled through the snow, nearer and nearer the house, articulating its long arms and legs like the appendages of a dreadful insect.

Suddenly, another form appeared, this time from the direction of the house. A man wearing a long coat was walking toward the creature, and in moments I recognized him as Duncan. I almost cried out to warn him of the creature's presence, but it was quickly apparent that he was actually heading straight for it. Trudging through the deep snow, he took perhaps half a minute to reach it. When he did so, he bent down and helped it raise itself on its legs. His back concealed it from me at first, then, as he moved to one side in order to assist it, I saw it stand erect. And though it was still too far from me to see more than the outline, I saw that it wore a long dress and that its hair fell almost to the ground.

I pulled the window down and let the curtains fall across it. In the darkness, I could hear my own breath rasping.

I DID NOT SLEEP AGAIN that night. In the morning, before breakfast, I looked out of my window again.

The sky was thick with cloud, and I could tell that more snow had come. Whatever tracks had been left on the meadow had been obliterated by a fresh fall.

Chapter

16

DUNCAN DROVE ME BACK after breakfast. Once we reached the main roads, the going was easy. Ploughs had been out already, and the sun had already melted the top surface of the snow. We parted at the entrance to Bakehouse Close. Duncan had work waiting for him at the law courts, and I said I wanted to put some notes in order before visiting the library.

In fact, I wanted to go to bed in order to catch up on the sleep I had lost the night before. I was still profoundly unsettled by what I had seen. The image of that curious, misshapen creature in the snow went ahead of me everywhere. I tried with little success to convince myself that it had, after all, been no more than a dream or a hallucination. Snow had not covered the creature's tracks, for there had never been any to cover. So I reassured myself.

I did sleep, but not well. My curtains were not thick enough to keep out a measure of daylight. From time to time, traffic sounds drifted in from the street. And sometimes, on waking, I was sure I could hear sounds in the empty space above me.

DURING THE NEXT FEW DAYS, I stayed out as much as possible, and did not answer my phone when it rang. I wanted time alone, to think things over and to decide what to do next. It was still not too late to look for a job, even if it meant leaving Edinburgh. My faith in Duncan had been shaken, yet the thought of a complete break left me breathless and frightened. The truth was that I had become psychologically dependent on Duncan. You haven't met him, you can't guess the force of that personality. He was my drug, and I needed a regular fix.

I went for long walks, out to Arthur's Seat and Lauriston Crags. There was snow underfoot, and a cold wind constantly in my face, but that was better than staying indoors brooding, waiting for night sounds outside my door. I thought a lot about Catriona, how she would have disapproved of what I had become involved in, calling it a waste of time or worse. I disapproved of it myself, in my rational mind; but I was not being rational, I was behaving like an addict for whom the decision to give up still seems like the most difficult thing imaginable.

In the end I grew tired. My thoughts seemed aimless and confused after the directed pursuits in which I had been engaged. I could not justify my behavior in ignoring Duncan: had he not treated me with extraordinary kindness, paying for my trip to Morocco, allowing me to keep on my flat, giving up hour upon hour of his valuable time merely to instruct me in the knowledge I was so eager to acquire? I went back to my flat and rang him at his office.

He did not ask where I had been, did not say he had been trying to get in touch with me. There was no suggestion that I was anything but a free agent, no hint that I might be answerable to him in some way. I thanked him for his hospitality.

"Nonsense," he said, "it was a pleasure to have you there. You must come again soon. It gets very dull in the countryside sometimes."

There was a pause. I waited. This was an awkward moment, for I felt we could not just continue as we had been.

"I'm glad you rang when you did," Duncan went on. "Are you free this evening?"

I said I was. He had not needed to ask.

"Excellent. You may remember that, when we first talked about your studies, I said I would introduce you to some friends of mine, people further along the path then yourself. I think the time has come. Get yourself ready for seven o'clock, I'll pick you up."

HE DROVE ME TO CLAREMONT PLACE, on the border between Pilrig and the New Town. It was a clear night, the moon less full than it had been at

Penshiel House, but bright for all that, hanging lazily in a sky without clouds. Duncan had said nothing to me of where we were headed. I expected a terraced house or a small clubhouse, at most a setup like that in Ainslie Place, perhaps part of a Georgian house touched by Duncan's wealth. I was not prepared for the reality.

The tower came in sight before we reached our destination, high, lifted up above the roofs, tall and black, as though light had never touched it. The moonlight appeared to slide off it, or to be swallowed by the stone. There could be no question, even at this distance: this was the church of my dreams.

Duncan parked on the opposite side of the road. We stepped out of the car and he led me across the street. The tall doorway stood where it had always stood in my dreams, waiting silently for me to come. I had to force myself to continue walking toward it, it was a struggle not to turn and run, to keep on running until I was free of that terrible place forever. Except that I knew deep down that running while awake would be no more use than running while asleep, that I could never break free of my nightmare simply by turning my back on it and all that it contained.

At first glance it seemed that the church was derelict, that it had not been in liturgical or other use for some time. The signs of neglect were visible everywhere, from boarded-up windows to broken or slipping masonry. Scaffolding had been erected at one side to carry out repairs, but it did not appear that anyone had worked there for years. A section of one wall was held in place by wooden buttresses.

And yet, for all the neglect, the building had lost none of its power. It had been designed to communicate a sense of religious awe, and that remained in the sheer scale with which it towered over the passerby. But it possessed something else, something I had felt the first time I saw it in my dream: a sense of brooding evil so overpowering that it took the breath away. There was a force in the very fabric of the building, a strength of purpose, as though the stones themselves had been imbued with a malign and ancient consciousness. Even without setting foot inside, I could feel that same presence of fear and loathing and brutality that I had sensed in the temple beneath d'Hervilly's house in Tangier.

"Is something wrong, Andrew?" Duncan asked as we started to climb the short flight of steps that led to the main door.

I was tempted to say, "No, of course not, everything's fine," but I could no longer bring myself to do so. I was afraid, really afraid this time, and no pretence could wipe it away.

"Yes," I said. "I've been here before. In my sleep."

"Of coure you have," said Duncan without hesitation. "You are neither the first nor the last. We have all dreamed of being here. This place is a focus, a beacon, a brightness."

"But they were terrible dreams, nightmares . . ."

He nodded.

"I expect they were. You can tell me about them later. I said this place is a focus. It acts as a prism for our emotions, it amplifies them, alters them. Some dream of what they most hope for, others of what they most fear. Don't be alarmed by that. Now you are here, the dreams will change. You will learn how to overcome your fears, how to use them for your own benefit and the good of others."

He smiled and took my arm.

"Come on, Andrew. Nothing awful will happen. You're perfectly safe with me."

From the outside, not a fragment of light had been visible through the boarded-up windows. Entering, I saw that candles had been lit in tall sconces along the aisles and in the chancel. They flickered in long, evenly spaced rows, barely touching the thick shadows that lay on every side and high above. I felt my heart freeze over like the surface of a pool that icy wind has crossed. This was, in every detail, though smaller in scale, the dark cathedral of my dreams, and all it lacked was the sound of voices chanting.

Ahead of us, gathered at the chancel end, was a group of half a dozen figures wearing hoods. At any moment, I thought, they would break into that abominable singing, and when they turned their faces would be pale and eyeless. But they did turn then, and when they pulled back their hoods, they looked just like anybody else.

Duncan introduced us, one at a time. Colin Baines, a bank manager; Alan Nesbitt, a venture capitalist with offices in Charlotte Square; James Partridge, an executive with BBC Scotland; Trevor McEwan, the chairman of a pharmaceuticals company; Paul Askew, a consultant in public relations;

Peter Lambert, one of Edinburgh's leading insurance brokers.

I saw at once that they had several things in common. They were all men, they were successful and fairly wealthy, and they belonged to the same class as Duncan. Not one of them had a Scottish accent. I remembered the people I had met in Tangier, and I asked myself again why Duncan took such an interest in me.

"Andrew, I'd like you just to sit and watch this evening. Do you mind?"

I shook my head.

"It won't be long before you're ready to take part," he went on. "But I'd like you to settle in first."

There was a chair near the choir stalls. I sat down, glancing nervously round me at the swaying shadows. On my right, there was a heavy door. Without being told, I knew it must lead to a subterranean crypt. I noticed that it was not wholly shut.

Duncan looked at his watch.

"Gentlemen, I think we should begin."

He took a robe from a cupboard and put it on. The altar had been removed from the chancel, and a large pentacle painted in the space it had occupied, framing a red circle. Duncan stepped into the center of this arrangement. The others pulled their hoods up and stood in a circle along the perimeter.

Duncan began to chant in Arabic. Hearing him, I realized that this had been the language of the liturgy I had heard in my dreams. His friends responded in the same language, and I recognized from snatches that they were using a text from which I had been taught by Sheikh Ahmad in Fez. Listening to their voices rise and fall, I had to fight to keep my growing panic down. I knew that, if I were to close my eyes, I would believe myself trapped in my nightmare again.

The chanting continued. There was nothing absurd about it, nothing preposterous in these respectable Edinburgh citizens dressed in robes and reciting magical texts in an abandoned church. Quite the contrary. The longer they chanted, the more sonorous grew their voices, the more controlled and purposeful their gentle swaying movements. The stone walls echoed to the carefully modulated rhythms of the chant, the Arabic words rolled through the church, calling, summoning, imploring. "Come," they chanted, "come. Make haste and come among us. Come. We are waiting, we are waiting. Come."

And something came. Their movements slowed, their breathing steadied, their voices deepened. They knew that a presence had come among them. Petrified, I felt it. Duncan's voice rose again and again, a note of triumph in it now. I heard a slithering sound behind me. Unable to stop myself, I looked round. The door of the crypt had moved. The sound was coming from behind it and, as I watched, something thin and white appeared in the gap.

I could bear it no longer. Frightened beyond measure, I leapt from the chair and ran down the nave. No one stopped me. Behind me, the voices continued uninterrupted. "Come," they chanted, "come." I reached the door and ran outside and kept on running, but the voices would not leave me, however far I went.

Chapter 17

DUNCAN RANG ME THE FOLLOWING morning, apologetic.

"I should have not have taken you," he said. "I thought you were ready, but clearly you need more preparation. Try not to worry about what happened, it's part of growing in the craft. You have yet to learn how to dominate your fears, how to prevent them taking over and coloring what you see and hear."

We talked for a little, Duncan explaining his theories about the power of the mind over place. But I did not believe him. What had happened in Morocco, what I had seen in Penshiel House, and what I had heard and witnessed the night before in the church left me with no choice. I could no longer believe in Duncan's high-mindedness, I could not take a step further down the path on which he was leading me. But I did not know how to break away.

It was Duncan himself who gave me the opportunity.

"Andrew, I have to go away for a week or so. There's some important business I have to attend to in London. It won't wait, and I can't send anyone in my place. We'll talk properly when I come back. I'll give you a ring."

"Have a good trip, Duncan. I'll see you when you get back."

But I had already decided what to do. I would not be there when he returned.

A CHANCE MEETING WITH ONE of my former students from New College put me on the track of a new place to live, a small flat in Drumdryan Street, in Tollcross, which a friend of his had just vacated. It was much cheaper than my current rooms, but, better than that, it was well away from Duncan's normal haunts. Though I lost a month's rent by doing so, I gave my notice and moved in to my new lodgings the next day.

As soon as I closed the door, I felt almost giddy with relief. It was as though the simple act of moving had served to wake me from a nightmare I had been almost unaware I was dreaming. I thought of Morocco and the events I had witnessed there with revulsion, and in my relief I vowed to have no more to do with Duncan or the dark world he inhabited.

At the same time, the more I felt free from his

influence, the more incredible some of my earlier fears began to seem. On the cold gray streets of Edinburgh, much of what had taken place that summer seemed incredible—the result of fancy or self-alienation or drugs. Men did not live for centuries, the dead did not wake in the mornings to go on with life, it was not possible to kill at a distance without mechanical means. So I reasoned.

I had been in my new quarters a week when I admitted to myself that it was time to visit Harriet. She had been much on my mind since my return, but until now I had been almost paralyzed by my feelings of guilt about Iain's death. My newfound rationality scattered all such notions, and I now felt greater guilt at having neglected her for so long. I telephoned right away, and this time Harriet herself answered.

There was a long silence when she heard my voice, as though I were someone she had thought lost or dead and never hoped to hear from again.

"I got your letter," I said. "I rang from Fez, but you were away. Someone else answered; a woman."

"That was my mother. She said someone had called without giving a name. I thought it might have been you."

"I'm back in Edinburgh. Can I come to see you?"

She paused, and for a moment or two I thought she was about to say no. But I was mistaken. She wanted to see me, there were things she had to talk with me about. Could I come that afternoon?

*　　*　　*

I TOOK A BUS TO DEAN VILLAGE. Harriet was waiting for me with tea and cake, just like the old days. She had just arrived home from school. A pile of dog-eared exercise books sat on the table, ready for marking. A copy of the collected poems of Eliot lay open on the arm of a chair by the fireplace.

She had changed. Physically, her face was thinner and there were gray streaks in her hair that had not been there before. More striking was the alteration in her manner. The brightness that had once impressed and cheered me had dimmed, and I was left with an abiding impression of sadness. Sadness, and what I took to be anger, not very far beneath the surface. She simultaneously comforted and frightened me.

"Thank you for coming," she said. "I knew you would in the end."

"I'm sorry, I should have come before this."

"There's no need to apologize. You say you got my letter?"

"It reached me in Tangier."

"Tangier? How very exotic that sounds. I wrote it just before . . . Iain's death. You were away so long—I had no other means of contacting you."

"I should have come back. Seen Iain, talked with him."

"No, why should you? It wouldn't have made any difference."

She lifted the pot and poured two cups of tea, Earl Grey in china cups, milk for her, lemon for myself. Thin slices of Dundee cake lay on the plates. Tangier and Fez and Marrakesh, Duncan Mylne and Sheikh Ahmad and the comte d'Hervilly all grew suddenly remote, components of a world I no longer inhabited, wiped out by the ordinariness of tea and cake.

"How did it happen?" I asked. "You said very little in your letter."

"There was little enough to say. It started a day or two after Iain went to visit you. He came back that evening quite upset. About what was happening to you, about this man Mylne. He'd asked around a bit more, found out things about Mylne that he didn't like. Anyway, a couple of days after seeing you he had the most blinding headache. It was gone by the next day, but I was really worried about him that night. Nothing had the least effect on the pain. He was awake all night, and at one point I found him in the kitchen, crying, it was so bad."

I could see that she was growing upset, reliving Iain's illness.

"Harriet, you don't have to go on. You've been through enough."

She looked up at me suddenly, catching a tear with a finger grown skillful over the past months.

"Enough? Really? You think there's a point at which someone says 'that's enough, you can feel better now'? Well, there isn't, because it just goes on and on, getting worse. It's not like prison, you know, you don't have a day or an hour when they come along and say, 'that's it, your time's up, you've done your stretch, you're free to go now.'"

I looked at her gently.

"Yes," I said, "I know."

Her eyes widened.

"I'm sorry, Andrew. I just forgot. You know what it's like as well as I do."

"Well enough," I said. I smiled. "It doesn't matter. I haven't been a very good friend to you this year."

"Let's forget about all that, Andrew. The chief thing is you're here."

She looked thoughtful.

"It is all over, isn't it?"she asked. "Mylne and everything?"

I hesitated. I had not really thought about it in such stark terms; but now the question had been put directly, I realised that was just how matters stood.

"Yes," I said, "I think so. I've decided to break with Duncan. I don't plan to see him again if I can help it."

"I'm glad to hear that. Iain worried about you a lot in the last weeks. His headaches kept coming back, and he started losing weight. They did all sorts of tests, but nothing seemed to come back positive.

"In between the headaches he wrote a long letter to you. He never let me see what was in it, or even so much as look at it; but he told me several times it was vital you read it."

"I see. Was this why you wanted me to come back?"

She nodded.

"Yes. Iain was very disturbed in his mind, as though something was haunting him. There was a dream that kept troubling him. He would call out in his sleep, night after night. I tried to talk with him about it, but he would say nothing. 'I need to speak to Andrew, I must speak to Andrew'—that was all he would say. I thought your being here might calm him down."

"I'm sorry. If I'd known sooner . . . "

"I don't think it would have done much good in the end. You couldn't have saved his life, no one could have done that. Perhaps your being here would have made him easier in his mind, it's hard to tell. But it might as easily have worsened his condition."

"You've no idea what was in his mind?"

She shook her head. Her gestures were wooden and somehow charmless. I understood. Grief is not ennobling.

"What about this letter? Did he finish it?"

"I don't know," she said. "If he did, I haven't been able to find it. I looked everywhere after he died, when I was going through his things, but there was no sign of it anywhere."

"Could he have posted it to me?"

"That's possible. Early on, he was still going out in between bouts of illness. It was only later that he was forced to stay indoors. They took him in to the Royal Infirmary at the end. That's where he died."

This time the bonds she had fashioned for herself did not hold. Her hand started trembling, and she put her cup down quickly, spilling tea across the table. I looked on helplessly as she doubled over, huddling against the force of the thing inside her. It passed slowly, as I had known it would, retreating back into its little black lair, gathering strength for the next time and the next.

"It was a very painful death," she said without apology. "Even with sedation, he suffered a great deal. The post mortem results were ambiguous. Whole sections of his brain were scarred, but they could find no cause for the injuries, no obvious agent. But it's over now. Knowing won't bring Iain back."

We mopped up the spilled tea and I poured a fresh cup for her. Her hand had steadied again.

"I'll look for the letter," I said. "He may have sent it to the department. Or to Tangier. There must be a way of getting it back if it's there."

"Perhaps," she said, but I could see that she no longer wanted to talk about it.

"Have you been to church much since . . . Iain died?"

She shook her head.

"I went at first," she said. "I thought it would help. It always had done in the past. But nothing anyone said made sense any longer. I don't go much now, I don't feel in harmony with it. My old church friends are shocked, of course. And perhaps they're right, perhaps I'll change again."

We went on talking until the cake had been eaten and the teapot drained. Outside, it had started to grow dark.

"I'd better be going," I said. "I'll get a bus on Queensferry Road."

As I got up, I knocked the copy of Eliot from the armchair. I picked it up and made to replace it. It had fallen open at *The Waste Land*. As I lifted it, my eye caught a passage on the right-hand page.

Who is the third who walks always beside you?
When I count, there are only you and I together
But when I look ahead up the white road
There is always another one walking beside you
Gliding wrapt in a brown mantle, hooded . . .

I shut the book and handed it back to Harriet. She had seen what I was reading.

"That was Iain's dream," she said. "A hooded figure luring him to something terrible. It's what he said in his sleep. He would never speak of it in daylight."

Chapter

18

IN THE COURSE OF OUR CONVERSATION, Harriet asked if I had been in touch with my parents. The truth was that I had neglected them badly, writing seldom and telephoning not at all. I had sent a short letter from Morocco, but it might as well have been penned by a stranger, so remote were its contents from the reality I was then living. Since my return, I had given priority to sorting out my life in Edinburgh and had avoided making contact with home.

Harriet's enquiry helped me make my mind up. That same evening, I made my way to a call box on Home Street and dialed their number.

My mother answered. I spoke to her in Gaelic, as though it would soften the shock.

"This is Andrew," I said. "I'm back in Edinburgh."

I held my breath. She was the strongest of the

cords pulling me back to reality. I needed her then more than I could say.

"Andrew. It's wonderful to hear from you. We were getting worried something had happened to you out in Africa."

"No," I said, "I'm all right. I got back a few weeks ago; but I wanted to wait until things settled down before getting in touch. How are you both?"

And so we began to talk of everyday life. Like Harriet's tea and cakes, my mother's island gossip chased the shadows farther from me. Life in Stornoway continued as before, marked by only minor changes: an elder of the kirk had died, a baby had been born to one of my cousins, an Indian family had arrived from the mainland and opened a shoe shop in the main street. That was the most exotic thing, and scarcely unusual.

My money ran out and she rang me back. There was no one else waiting.

I said little about Morocco, portraying the summer as little more than a mixture of holiday and research.

"I'm glad to be home," I said. "I stayed away too long."

"I'm glad you're well, dear," she said. "Perhaps we'll see you soon. Now, I know your father would like a word with you."

I heard the handset put down, then footsteps and muffled voices. Moments later, my father came on the line.

"Andrew, it's good to hear your voice."

He asked about my job, and I told him I was waiting for something else to turn up.

"Why don't you come to Stornoway?" he asked. "You could spend the winter here, save a fortune on heating bills."

"Thanks," I said, "but I'd rather stay on. I need to sort things out here first. Going home would be . . . well, it would be an easy way out. I don't think it's a good idea. Maybe when I'm more settled. I might be able to get over for Christmas."

"That's a good idea. But, look, would you have any objection to my coming over? I have some leave due, I could be with you next week."

My first impulse was to say no, but I checked myself. Why not, after all? It would be good for me to see my father. I badly needed his unshakable skepticism.

"Yes," I said, "I'd like that very much. Why don't you both come? I can't put you up, but there are plenty of guest houses round here."

I gave him my new address. I was already looking forward to their visit.

"Andrew, before you go, there's one wee thing I have to mention. While you were away, a man from Glasgow City Council got in touch. He'd been trying to contact you. I told him you were in Morocco, but that I'd speak to you as soon as you got in touch. He'd like you to ring him sometime. His name's McPherson, I have his number here."

"Do you know what it's about?"

"Well, he wouldn't tell me. But I think it's to do with Catriona's grave. I have a feeling it's been vandalized."

"You'd better give me this man's number. I'll ring him in the morning."

*   *   *

JAMIE MCPHERSON WORKED for the parks and cemeteries division of the council. He sounded relieved
when I explained who I was.

"Dr. Macleod, I'm so glad you've finally got in
touch. I did write to you at your university department and Tangier, but I don't suppose you had my
letters."

"No, my father told me you spoke to him."

"That's right. He said he'd ask you to ring as
soon as he heard from you."

"What's it about? Father thought it might be to
do with my wife's grave."

There was a silence of several seconds during
which he assumed his official manner.

"Yes," he said, his voice lower now and more
solemn, "that's correct. There's been . . . " I heard
him hesitate, imagined him choosing his words
carefully. "There's been some trouble. From time to
time we have vandalism in the cemeteries. It's
mostly young louts on a Saturday night. They'll be
passing by a cemetery, then one dares another to
climb the wall. After that it gets a bit out of hand.
They kick over a headstone or two, maybe smash
some ornaments. Last year we found graffiti on
some Jewish graves. Swastikas and so on."

"Her headstone's been vandalised, is that what
you're trying to tell me?"

"Well, as a matter of fact, no. It's worse than
that. Her grave was dug up one night in August.
I'm sorry to have to tell you this, but your wife's
remains have been stolen."

*   *   *

I TOOK THE NEXT TRAIN to Glasgow and spent the rest of the day shuttling between the council offices and the main police station. The incident had taken place on the night of the nineteenth of August. Diggers had found the grave opened and the coffin gone the next morning, on arriving to start their day's work.

A police investigation had started immediately, but so far they had drawn a complete blank. Grave robbing was sufficiently rare to leave the entire Glasgow police force perfectly helpless. This was not a crime like drug pushing or rape. There were no clues, no lists of suspects with previous convictions, no informers ready to spill the beans for a few pounds. The investigation had centered on youth gangs who might have dug up a grave for kicks, a few would-be satanists, and a student group at the university called the Burke and Hare Club.

I thought it diplomatic to say nothing of my precise research interests. For the record, I described myself as a sociologist and left it at that. Needless to say, I told them nothing of my own suspicions, if they even qualified as such.

I knew that Duncan could not have been personally involved. But he had friends whom he might have persuaded to carry out something of the kind. All I knew was that the nineteenth of August was the day I left Fez for Marrakesh, the day after my last session with Sheikh Ahmad. I remembered my words to him on that occasion: "Catriona is dead. Her body is in a grave, rotting."

* * *

ON RETURNING TO EDINBURGH, I had just enough time to visit my old department in the university. The secretary had stayed on late to finish some typing, and I asked if any mail had been sent to me over the summer. There were some bits and pieces, most of them internal memos about seminars and public lectures. I opened everything, but Iain's letter was not among them.

I had not slept well since my return, and that night sleep refused to come for several hours. I had not visited Catriona's grave, there would have been no point—it had been filled in again and the headstone replaced. But try as I might, I saw the robbery enacted again and again in my mind's eye, the diggers arriving after midnight, hooded men without eyes, tearing at the soil until they reached the coffin, lifting it from its resting place, slipping away under cover of darkness with their prize.

A little before dawn I began to sleep. There were no dreams at first, just images drawn from the thoughts that had been tormenting me through the night.

And then, as though a curtain had been raised, I found myself dreaming, yet fully conscious of everything I saw and heard. I was walking by night down a steep, narrow street in a strange city. From the curved archways and heavy wooden doors on either side, I guessed at once that it was either Fez or another city in North Africa.

The winding street descended ever more steeply toward the heart of the city, but however far I walked I never saw another human being. All about me was silent and deserted, the dark, brooding facades of the blind houses on both sides, the forbidding aspect of the black alleyways that branched at regular intervals off the main street. I had no idea where I was headed, but I knew that something deep in the darkness was drawing me, waiting for me.

I passed the gate of an ancient mosque bearing an inscription over its portal in Kufic lettering. Several yards past it, a narrow opening to the right led into a dark, poorly paved alley. My feet turned into it as though by some instinct of their own, taking me farther into the maze of the city.

Without warning, there appeared in the darkness ahead of me a tall hooded figure wearing a white jellaba. He was standing with his back to me, still and somehow sinister. As I drew near, he turned around slowly. His face was shrouded in the wide hood, and I could make out nothing of his features. I wanted to turn and run from him, but my legs would not let me. Instead, I felt myself compelled to walk nearer and nearer to the man in front of me. As I came within a few feet of him, he lifted his hands and started to pull the hood back from his face. It fell completely away and he stepped forward into a shaft of moonlight.

I woke screaming. It was early morning, and I was lying in my own bed, the sheets twisted as though in a frenzy. My body was viscous with sweat, and I was shivering.

I pulled the blankets round me and huddled against the pillows, trying to get warm. Thin sunlight struggled through my window. I could hear cars outside, and the voices of excited children playing hopscotch. A dog barked at the end of the street. An airplane passed by slowly overhead. My heart began to slow. The images of the dream inside my head were receding. But something in the room was wrong.

I strained my ears, but could hear nothing but the sounds from outside. My eyes, adjusted to the dim light, could see nothing out of the ordinary. But I knew something was not as it should be.

And then, just as I had decided that it was all imagination and was preparing to get out of bed, I knew what it was. I could smell perfume. It was faint, but unmistakable. I knew its name at once: Jicky. It had been Catriona's favorite scent.

Chapter

19

I COULD NOT BEAR TO STAY in my rooms. The thought of remaining indoors to inhale that perfume was repugnant to me. Outside, late autumnal sunshine lay folded across the street like yellow gauze. I slipped on a coat and went out, having no other aim in mind than to get away for a while.

During my mother's visit, she and I had gone more than once to the Botanical Garden in Inverleith, and it now seemed to me the ideal place to chase away the shadows of the night. A bus took me to Canonmills, and from there it was a short stretch to the garden.

I spent the morning there, strolling among the flower beds or sitting by the lake. All around me were families come for a Saturday outing, laughing children, students, lovers—the ordinary world going about its business. It was the world I was desperately reaching to regain, but I felt shut out from it as though by a thin, impermeable glass.

I had a light lunch in the café. Outside, it had grown a little cloudy, and I thought of returning home. The thought of it depressed me. I needed to see someone, to talk over what had been happening. Remembering that it was a only short bus ride from Inverleith to Dean Village, I found a telephone and rang Harriet. She was at home and, yes, she would like to see me. There was something she wanted me to look at.

"Let's go out," she said when I arrived. "I can't stand being cooped up in here all the time." I remembered that she and Iain used to spend their weekends going for long walks together. She must have been miserable on her own, now that the freshness of Iain's death had worn off and her friends had discovered other things to do with their Saturdays.

We took our time, walking slowly beside the stream that runs through the village on its way to the sea at Leith, beneath Dean Bridge and down to St. Bernard's Well. The sky had cleared a little, filling from time to time with circling flocks of migratory birds preparing for their journey south to Africa. They seemed ill-omened creatures, poised there above us, as though waiting to carry news of me into places I preferred to forget.

I told Harriet about the incident at Catriona's grave, and from that passed to the perfume I had smelled, or fancied I smelled, that morning. It was but a short step from there to unburdening myself about Duncan Mylne and the events of the summer. I stopped short of blaming Mylne for Iain's death, and said nothing of my discovery of the scarf; but I think she had already guessed that something of the sort had been going through my mind.

I expected her to make light of everything, to find ways in which to explain my fears away. But, as I talked, I noticed her grow steadily more serious. The banter with which we had tried to cheer one another when we started out was now dropped. We were in the midst of grim events.

"I don't expect you to believe much of this," I said when I had reached the end of my account.

"On the contrary," she replied, "it makes a great deal of sense. I'd like to say it's all nonsense, but I don't think it is. Iain said some things to me before he died; they worried me a lot. And since then . . ."

She hesitated, and I guessed she was coming to the nub of what she wanted to say. We had reached the well and turned back. The last traces of sunshine had been wiped from the sky by fresh clouds. The surface of the stream beside which we walked was flat and colorless.

"I wanted to show you this," she said. She reached into her coat pocket and drew out a rectangular piece of card. As she turned it to hand it to me, I saw that it was a photograph.

"This is myself and Iain," she said. "It was taken on our wedding day six years ago."

She passed it over. Her hand was shaking gently. A flock of large black birds passed over us like a stain. One cried out bleakly, as though its heart was broken.

They were dressed in wedding clothes. My eye caught sight of Harriet first, her veil pulled back, a bouquet of roses and irises in her hand, her lips parted, her face shining. Beside her stood a thin, bent man who was, I guessed, her father. But then I looked closer and saw that it was Iain.

"I don't understand," I said. "Are you saying Iain was already ill when you married him? That the illness he died from was a recurrence of something he'd had before?"

She shook her head.

"When that photograph was taken," she said slowly, "Iain looked as healthy as he did when you first met him. If anything, healthier. I found this after he died, when I was looking through our photograph albums. And not just this. Every photograph I have of him has changed. As though he had always been days away from death."

I stared down at the photograph, unable to comprehend.

"Surely it's not possible," I said.

"How possible were any of those things you've just finished telling me about?"

I handed the photograph back to her and we walked on. I thought of Duncan and the comte d'Hervilly, how they had fingered my photographs of Catriona. But Catriona had been dead and beyond their reach. What then had been the purpose of all that, and why had they troubled to have her body disinterred?

"I can't do anything now for Iain," I said. "But

I have to find a way to put an end to all this for myself. And you—you may be in danger too."

"If I were still active in the Church," said Harriet, "I'd suggest an exorcism, or whatever it is they do in these cases. But I no longer know what to think. I prayed for Iain night and day, the whole congregation prayed for him, but it didn't save his life. I think that this is something beyond the reach of ordinary prayers."

"Is there anyone in the church you could still speak to? Even if ordinary prayers won't work, perhaps there's something else."

"I don't know. Maybe. I'll have to think about it. What about you? Will it be enough just to stay out of Mylne's way?"

I shrugged. I had not really thought much further than that. Keeping away from Duncan certainly seemed the essential thing. But perhaps I could do more.

"I still have my books," I said. "The ones I bought, and a few Duncan gave me. Maybe I should get rid of them."

"That seems like a good idea. Get rid of everything. Your notes, photographs, anything linked to that business. If you cut yourself off entirely, there'll be no way Mylne or anyone else can get through to you."

We reached her door. She invited me in again for tea, but I reckoned she had seen enough of me for one day.

"I'd better be getting back," I said. "The sooner I get to work sorting all that stuff out, the better. When can I see you again?"

"I'm sorry, but I have to be away for a few days. I promised my parents-in-law I'd spend the half-term break with them in St. Andrews. They've booked us into a hotel for the week. I was to have gone today, but there were things I wanted to get straightened out here first. You're lucky you found me in."

"When do you get back?"

"Not till next Saturday. I want to have Sunday to myself: I need a proper rest before going back to work on Monday. My mother's very keen on walks. But I'll ring round a couple of people I know from the church, see what they think. Ring me on Saturday evening and I'll tell you if I have anything."

"You don't have to stay involved with this, Harriet. I brought it on myself, I have to deal with it alone."

She shook her head.

"This matters to me," she said. "I want to help. Please don't shut me out again."

I remembered how I had treated her in the spring.

"No," I said, "I won't. I promise."

I TOOK A BUS BACK TO TOLLCROSS. Still new to the area, I stayed on too long, getting off halfway up Bruntsfield Place. I would have to walk back.

Here, in a region of tenements dating from the last century, the buildings were old and grimy. A shabby pall hung over the street, decaying shop fronts and grime-choked windows denying both air and sunlight opportunity to pass. Depressed by the main road, I decided to take a more circuitous route through the side streets and alleys that meander through the district. I turned off at the next opening and was soon engulfed in a maze of narrow, unfamiliar streets, streets that seemed older and darker than their smart neighbors to the west.

There were few people about. Ordinarily, I would have found the quiet of a late Saturday afternoon relaxing, but here in these unknown, lifeless streets the silence and emptiness weighed on me. I began to feel jaded and alone. Out of forgotten corners, feelings of despair crept out to attack me. Everything seemed useless and far away from what I had once imagined life should be: Catriona was dead, my career in ruins, the future nothing but gray streets and washed-out buildings. The mastery of which I had dreamed so recently had already turned into a nightmare that threatened to destroy me utterly.

I kept on walking, sluggish with self-pity. What it was exactly that first drew my eye to the shop, I do not know. I had entered a small and gloomy cul-de-sac, thinking that it was a way back to a street I had left a few minutes earlier. I noticed a pub on the corner and thought I might go in for a drink; but as I turned, my attention was caught by a small leaded window flanking a low door on my left. The sign above was evidently old, covered with the accumulated dust and grime of years; I could make out neither name nor trade.

My curiosity was aroused by the oddness of a shop so little interested in attracting passing trade.

Approaching the window, which was dark and partly covered with cobwebs, I peered in. To my surprise, I could make out behind the dirt-caked glass several piles of dusty books; in the gloom of the shop beyond, a dim yellow light was burning. It seemed that I had stumbled across a secondhand bookshop so far off the beaten track that I had never even heard of it before.

Assuming it was closed, I turned to go, thinking I might return during the coming week to browse. But the thought of old books reminded me of my decision to get rid of my occult collection. This, surely, would be the ideal place. I would probably be paid pennies for them, but it would be better than destroying the books outright. I went back to the door to see if there was a card showing opening times. Seeing none, I tried the handle, and to my surprise it turned and the door opened.

Three shallow steps took me down to the floor. Its interior was poorly lit, and it took fully half a minute before my eyes could adjust to the gloom. The door closed on a spring behind me, banging gently. Beyond, I could see several shelves piled with books, and scattered everywhere across the floor were heaps of unsorted volumes and magazines. What wallpaper was visible was brown and yellowing, showing here and there patches of damp; in the corners and between portions of the shelves there hung black cobwebs. A musty, decaying smell filled the air.

It was such an uncheering scene that I had second thoughts about staying. Just then, however, a door at the rear of the shop opened and a stooped figure emerged. The proprietor was an old man wearing a faded purple dressing gown over gray trousers. His white hair hung loosely to rounded shoulders, and in his hands he held a black ivory-handled cane.

I had expected someone seedy, a shabby creature with dried egg stains on his waistcoat, an asthmatic drunkard already well into his second whisky bottle, an unshaven wreck with huge bags beneath his eyes. But there was nothing of that in the man before me, nothing lax, nothing careless, nothing down-at-heel. His eyes were bright blue and disturbingly direct; they seemed almost the eyes of a young man trapped in an old man's body. The face was deeply etched with wrinkles, and all about the eyes hung a sad, contemplative expression. A dark mole on his cheek contrasted with the pallor of skin that possessed the singular whiteness of antique ivory.

Leaning lightly on his cane, he came slowly to the front of the shop and stood facing me. I sensed neither welcome nor dismissal in his eyes and hurried to explain why I had come.

"I'm sorry if I've disturbed you," I said. "But the door was open and . . . "

"It's perfectly all right," he answered. "I always remain open late on Saturdays." He spoke with a strong English accent, and his voice was soft, a melodious and measured voice with a faint trace in it of . . . what? Menace? Disdain? I could not tell, yet when he spoke it both soothed and disturbed me. He went on speaking.

"It really makes little difference to me," he said. "I live on the premises. The shop is generally open when I am up and about, and closed at any other time. I have few visitors, few customers. From time to time I send out catalogues. Were you after anything in particular?"

"Well, I am a collector, but . . . " I hesitated. It was unlikely someone like this would want to burden his already overstocked shop with my rather obscure odds and ends. "The thing is," I went on, "that I have quite a few books I no longer have any use for. I wondered if you might be interested in looking at them. I live quite near here."

He tapped his cane on the floor. His eyes did not leave my face.

"What sort of books?"

I explained as well as I could, emphasising my research, playing down my own interest in the subjects in question. He listened attentively, and asked pertinent questions about certain of the titles I mentioned. He seemed to be familiar with the field.

"Well," he said when I had finished describing what I owned, "you have little of any merit. All common enough titles from the sound of it. But I don't doubt I could find room for them. Provided you aren't expecting much by way of return."

I shook my head.

"No, the money's scarcely important. I'd just like to get rid of them. My . . . research has moved into other areas, and I don't have enough room for everything."

"Well, come again soon and bring some of them with you. I'm sure we can do a deal. And by all means have a look round. You may find something of interest."

I thought of making my apologies and leaving, but it occurred to me that it might be worth a glance. During my visit on Thursday, Harriet had been talking about the trouble she had experienced finding good editions of some of Hardy's early novels. Shops like this often had decent nineteenth-century volumes.

Half an hour later, my expectations were realized. I found a copy of *Desperate Remedies*, one Hardy that I knew Harriet particularly wanted. The price penciled on the flyleaf was well within my reach, and I decided to take it.

The old man was sitting on an armchair at the back. I handed the book to him.

"You like Hardy?" he asked.

"It's for a friend," I said. I handed him four pounds.

"I'll wrap it for you. Just give me a moment."

He passed through the curtain that screened the back room from the shop proper, taking the book with him. A short time later, he reappeared, holding a well-wrapped parcel in one hand. Smiling, he handed it to me.

"This was the book you wanted, wasn't it?" he asked.

"Of course," I said, taking it from him. "Thank you. I'll come back next week with the other books."

"There's no hurry," he said. "When you're ready. Leave yourself time to have a proper look round. I keep my best books in the back."

He showed me to the door and told me the best way to get back to Tollcross. I set off, carrying my parcel under one arm, buttoning my coat against the chill of the coming night.

Chapter 20

THE FIRST THING I DID on arriving back in my rooms was to pack all my occult books together and put them in boxes in a cupboard on the landing. There was a sense almost of victory in doing so. I was putting the evil of the past year behind me, embarking on a new life in which there would be no room for shadows of any sort. I had started to look forward to my father's visit, and had already begun to think of looking for a new job. There would still be copies of the *Times* Higher Education Supplement on sale on Monday; I could pick one up and see what was on offer.

The scent of Jicky had vanished from the bedroom. I convinced myself that I must have imagined it after all. My studies had already persuaded me that there was much self-suggestion in the whole business of occult phenomena, and I could

readily believe that the previous day's unpleasantness had stirred up memories of Catriona that had
focused on one significant element.

At seven o'clock I went out and bought myself
some Chinese food in a nearby take-away. I had
just returned and was unwrapping the cartons
when someone rang my bell. Apart from Harriet
and my parents, no one knew my new address.

I went to the hall and picked up the intercom
handset.

"Yes?"

A man's voice answered.

"Is that Dr. Macleod?"

"Yes. What do you want?"

"It's the police, sir. Would you mind if we
came up? We need to speak to you."

For a moment I was thrown, but I had, after
all, spent much of the day before in a police station.

"Yes, that's all right. I'll let you in. I'm on the
top floor."

There were two of them, a man and a woman.
We sat at the table in the living room. They were a
few years younger than myself and seemed embarrassed. The woman cleared her throat.

"We're glad we caught you in, sir. We dropped
by earlier, but you were out."

"I went for a walk. I only got back a short time
ago."

"You're not on the telephone, so we were
asked to visit. Glasgow CID needs to talk to you."

"Is it about my wife's grave?"

"Yes, sir, it is. They'd like to see you tonight if
possible."

"Tonight? I can't get to Glasgow tonight."

"Apparently the grave has been opened again, sir. They want you to go over. They have something to show you. If you don't have your own transport, we can take you by car."

WE WERE IN GLASGOW half an hour later. My escort waited while I was taken to an interview room on the third floor. Five minutes later, the door opened and Inspector Cameron came in. He had taken me through the details of the case the day before.

"I'm sorry we've had to haul you back here so soon, Dr. Macleod. But the constable who picked you up in Edinburgh will have explained. Your wife's grave was opened again last night."

"You don't think I had anything to do with it, do you?"

He shook his head vehemently.

"Of course not. I just wanted you here to see if you could shed some light on what we found when we went out there this afternoon."

"What you found?"

"Aye, in the bottom of the grave. Whoever dug it up left something this time."

There was a knock and the door opened. A constable in shirtsleeves came in carrying a shallow cardboard box.

"Just put it on the table, Jimmy, and leave us," said Cameron.

When the door closed, Cameron approached the table, beckoning to me to accompany him.

"You needn't worry, Dr. Macleod, there's nothing unpleasant in the box. Just some wee things that are puzzling us."

He lifted the lid. Inside were half a dozen assorted objects, neatly arranged. I felt my heart shrink as I looked at them. One was an Arabic talisman, a triangular piece of brass engraved with a spell in crudely executed *naskh* characters. Beside it lay a sheet of paper inscribed with a European magic square, the text written in Latin. Next to that was a silver ring: I did not pick it up, but I knew it would bear a short inscription along the inside. A goat's hoof. A shallow bowl with traces of dried blood along the rim. A nail.

"Why are you showing me these?" I asked. "They mean nothing to me."

"Are you quite sure, sir?"

"Sure? Of course I'm sure. You're not suggesting I had anything to do with this?"

He shook his head, standing back against the wall.

"I know of no reason to suggest anything of the kind. I was just curious, that's all. You can guess what sort of thing they represent, though, can't you?"

I nodded. I was finding it hard to keep control of my voice.

"Something to do with black magic," I said. "Ritual objects, charms. You don't need me to tell you that."

"No, of course we don't, sir. It's just that . . . " He hesitated. I had to keep looking at him, I told myself that looking away would seem like an admission of guilt. "We understand your research brought you into contact with this sort of thing.

Magic. The occult. That is what you were researching, wasn't it, sir?"

I should have guessed they would ask around in order to find out what they could about me.

"'Not exactly, Inspector. At least, not in the way you suggest. I'm a sociologist. My work involved occult groups: their composition, meeting patterns, class structure, interconnections. I wasn't interested in what they actually did or taught. That was never my field of enquiry."

"I see. So you'd never have seen things like this in the course of your work?"

"In books perhaps. Never in the flesh."

"But you were involved with groups who might make use of things of this kind?"

I nodded. It seemed foolish to pretend otherwise. There were people at New College who could tell him the sort of groups I had examined.

"Yes, certainly, but—"

"In which case, we may have a motive for all this. Don't you think so, sir? Perhaps one of the groups you were investigating took exception to something you wrote about them. Is that at all possible?"

"Not that I know of. My relations with the subjects I studied were always amicable."

"You don't know of anyone you may have rubbed up the wrong way? They can be touchy, these occult types."

"Perhaps. It's possible that, without my knowing . . . "

"Exactly, sir. You wouldn't necessarily have known you'd offended them. This would be their way of passing on a message, as it were."

"A very unpleasant way."

"Yes, we think so too." He paused. "Will you sit down a moment, sir."

I took a chair and drew it up to the table. Cameron took a pack of cigarettes from his pocket. He held them out to me.

"Smoke?"

"No, thank you. Inspector, if this is all there is to it, perhaps it's best forgotten."

"Aye, maybe. But you're forgetting the matter of your wife's body. That's not so trivial. And there's something worse than that."

"Worse? I don't understand."

"That wasn't all we found in your wife's grave today." He put a cigarette between his lips and lit it. Smoke filled the still air between us.

"There was a child's body," he said. "A boy about a year old. We think he was buried alive.'

Chapter

21

I RANG HARRIET'S NUMBER first thing in the morning, but she had already gone. She had not left me a number or an address where I could contact her in St. Andrews. After what had happened, I badly needed to see her; she was the only person with whom I could talk openly about Mylne and his activities.

There had been noises during the night, in the space above my flat. They had stopped around dawn, but I had been unable to get back to sleep. I thought I might have dreams, and I feared what I might see were I to do so. It was about eight o'clock when I finally got up. The long day stretched ahead of me, purposeless, yet full of indefinable menace.

The weather had turned colder overnight, and walking outside seemed much less attractive than it had the day before. On a gloomy day, Edinburgh can be a black and depressing city, and I was badly in need of something to lift my spirits. On an impulse, I took a bus to Kelso and spent the day visiting Floors Castle. Its glories meant as little to me as the streets I had just left. Everywhere I went, I was accompanied by the memory of sounds I wanted to forget. But I was with other people, and their company got me through the day.

Arriving back at the bus station just after seven, I decided to ring my father, in the hope of persuading him to leave a day or two earlier. I needed his advice and support in this fresh dilemma.

My mother answered as before.

"Andrew, thank God you've rung. I wanted to get hold of you, but you aren't on the phone now, and I'd no idea how to get in touch."

I could tell at once that she was worried about something.

"What is it?" I asked. "Is something wrong?"

"It's your father," she answered. "He's been taken ill. Very ill, though Dr. Boyd can not say what the matter is. He woke in the middle of the night on Thursday, not long after you spoke to him, with the most dreadful headache. I gave him tablets, but they did no good, no good at all, and by morning he was much worse—doubled up and vomiting. I had the doctor in to him right away, and he tried a stronger painkiller. That helped a little, but the headache never left him all that day."

I listened, not knowing in my heart of hearts what I listened to. They were just words, I thought, I could ignore them if I pleased. I felt my skin grow cold, then hot, as though I had developed a fever.

All round me the noise of the bus station continued unabated, the clamor untouched by what my mother was saying far away on Lewis.

"He was better yesterday, and he's been well again today, but Friday took it out of him. He'll not be able to get to Edinburgh as he promised. Dr. Boyd is talking of sending him to the mainland for tests, to Inverness possibly."

"Wouldn't Edinburgh be the best place? It has some of the best hospitals in the country."

"Well, it might be. I would have to speak to the doctor about it. He doesn't want your father to travel far if it can be helped."

"Yes, I understand that. It's just that . . . " I realized it would be a mistake to tell my mother anything of the matters that were troubling me. She would not be able to offer help, and she had enough on her mind at the moment with my father's illness. I certainly could not tell her what his symptoms boded to me. "It's just that I had been looking forward to seeing him."

"Can't you come to Stornoway? You're not working now, and you could be a great help to me here."

I wanted more than anything to go there in order to be with my father. But as I was about to answer, I realized that travelling to Stornoway was out of the question. If Duncan had brought about my father's illness, just as he had done Iain's, it could only have been for one purpose: to prevent his coming to Edinburgh to see me. My arrival in Stornoway might very well prove my father's death warrant.

"I'm sorry," I said. "There's been bother here over this business with Catriona's grave. The police are carrying out an investigation, they want me to be available."

"That's shocking, Andrew. Was the grave badly damaged?"

"Just the headstone. I'm having it replaced."

"Where will you find the money? We'll be happy to send you some."

"Thanks, but there's no need. The insurance will take care of it." That was not true, I had never had the headstone insured, but I thought it best to keep my parents uninvolved.

"Give Father my love," I said. "Tell him I'm sorry he's not coming. Perhaps you can both come as soon as he's better. He'll need a holiday."

"Is there no way of getting in touch with you, Andrew? I'm worried. In case . . . anything happens."

"He'll be fine, you shouldn't worry. Look, I'll ring every night. And I'll look into getting a phone installed. I'll speak to you tomorrow."

I WALKED HOME, shaken and afraid. Questions buzzed through my brain like flies. How had Mylne known that my father planned to visit me? If he had used something belonging to my father in order to set his spell, how had he come by it? Had the fresh desecration of Catriona's grave been connected in some way to the attack on my father?

More than anything, I kept asking myself why it was that Mylne had left Harriet untouched until now. Was he unaware that we had been seeing one another? How could that be, if he knew about my father? And why was he so intent on acting against anyone who threatened in some way to come between him and myself?

I ate another badly cooked Chinese meal and played the television loudly, watching programs in which I had not the slightest interest merely to make company for myself and to put off the moment when I would be too tired to stay awake.

But not even the constant action of the television could interrupt the thoughts singing through my head. One thought in particular would not leave me alone. It returned to me again and again, and in the end I could stand it no longer. I got up and went to the filing cabinet in the corner. A drawer at the bottom contained two large photograph albums. I lifted them out and returned to my chair.

I knew what I was looking for, and I was not disappointed. The first album held all the photographs I had of my parents, including some taken the previous Christmas. In all of them, my father's face was that of a man newly stricken by sudden, inexplicable pain. He did not yet show the symptoms that had been so visible on Iain's face in the photograph Harriet had shown me. But the beginnings were there, and I knew that, if I continued to look at them, the photographs would soon betray his decline and eventual death.

The second album contained my photographs of Catriona. I only looked at one: it was enough, enough to haunt me for the rest of my life. I had expected to see her in the final stages of her illness, just as Harriet's photograph had shown Iain shortly before his death. But that was not how Catriona looked at all.

It was the first photograph taken of us together. My friend Jamie had posed us outside the Burrell, solemn for once, my arm round Catriona's shoulder. A steep northern light fell on us from behind.

The album slipped from my hands and fell to the floor with a crash. I closed my eyes, but the image would not leave them. What I had seen was simple but chilling: in the photograph Catriona was dressed in a long white garment. A hood covered her head and face. And my arm still lay where it had always lain, round her shoulder, pressing her to me.

Chapter
22

THE SOUNDS RETURNED THAT NIGHT again. Sometimes they came as far as my door, and I sat listening to them move about on the landing. After they grew silent, I retrieved my books from the cupboard and studied what I should do to protect myself. I prepared circles of defence against them and filled them with spells carefully recited and drawn, but I had no confidence in them.

Still shaken by what I had found in the photograph album, I went to a nearby café for breakfast. On the way I stopped in a newsagent's to buy a copy of the *Times* Higher Educational Supplement, and while there I picked up a copy of *The Scotsman* to read over breakfast.

The story was on the second page. Cameron had left out any reference to Catriona or myself, and he had said nothing about the talismans and other items found in the grave, but the rest of the details were there. The baby had been identified as Charles Gilmore, eleven months old, taken from his pram outside a shop in Airdrie on Friday afternoon. There was a photograph of the bairn in his mother's arms. Catriona's grave was not shown, and nothing was said about satanists or grave robbers. The text merely stated that the ground had been "disturbed."

On the way back to my rooms, I bought the morning tabloids, but they gave few more details and a great deal more speculation, none of it remotely accurate. I rang Cameron and asked if he had come up with anything since receiving confirmation of the baby's identity, but he said there was nothing yet.

"Say nothing to anyone," he told me. "If word gets out that a bunch of satanists are prowling Glasgow killing babies, there'll be an almighty panic."

"You don't have to worry. I've no intention of going to the press. And I sincerely hope this is the last killing."

There was a pause at the other end. The possibility of other murders must, I realized, be the inspector's nightmare.

"I hope so too, Dr. Macleod. If you think of anything you may have forgotten to tell us, get in touch."

As I put down the phone, I reached a snap decision. I would go to St. Andrews to look for Harriet. She would know what to do. St. Andrews is a very small town, and I reckoned that I could call on all the hotels there in a single afternoon.

I went back to my rooms to change and pick up some money for the trip. As I turned to go, I noticed the book I had bought for Harriet lying on the table where I had left it, still in its wrapper. I thought a present might help lighten our meeting. Picking the book up, I slipped it into my coat pocket.

On arriving at the central bus station, I found that the next bus for St. Andrew's left in half an hour. I bought a ticket and waited. We left on time, heading north over the Forth Bridge, then east to the coast. Two hours later, I was at my destination. A cold wind was brawling in from the sea, and the streets were filled with students scurrying to lectures. The university dominated the small town, lending it an unreal air, like a film set inhabited by aliens.

I found the tourist information office and obtained a map and a list of all the town's hotels. In the end, it did not prove as difficult as I had feared. I remembered that Harriet had once mentioned that her father-in-law was keen on golf, and it occurred to me that he would most probably have chosen a hotel near one of the courses. I found them at Rusack's, right alongside the eighteenth fairway of the Old Course, in the dining room, having lunch.

Harriet made her apologies and we went together to the lounge.

"This is a lovely surprise," she said. "My father-in-law can be rather boring this close to a golf course. It's a relief to be snatched away. But I think I'll have some explaining to do. A strange man coming all the way from Edinburgh to see me!"

"I had to come," I said.

Her mood immediately grew serious.

"Has something happened?" she asked.

I showed her the piece in *The Scotsman*.

"I read this this morning," she said. "I don't see what . . . " She stopped and looked at me in horror. "Don't tell me it was Catriona's grave."

I told her all about my interview with Cameron.

"Why didn't you tell him about Mylne?" she asked.

"What would have been the point? I have no real evidence, nothing that would stand up in a court of law. Mylne won't have been anywhere near Glasgow on Friday night, and he wasn't even in this country when the grave was first opened."

"But we know he's behind this."

"I'm certain of it. If we could find evidence to connect him to the child's murder, I wouldn't hesitate to pass it on. But I don't think it will happen. I think we have to go about this in our own way."

"What do you want me to do?"

"I'd like you to come back to Edinburgh. If you have friends there who might be able to help, we should be seeing them now."

"Oh, Andrew, I don't know. . . . My parents-in-law will be hurt if I just get up and leave. They're finding Iain's death very hard: he was their only child. And I seriously think that leaving with a strange man could upset them badly. I wouldn't be able to explain, not adequately."

"Harriet, I have no one else to turn to."

"What about your own parents?"

I told her about my father. I had not intended

to, knowing how badly it would disturb her, but I needed to impress on her how things stood with me.

"You should have told me about this earlier," she said. "You're right, we have to do this together. Give me a few minutes with them, I'll do my best to explain."

"You can't tell them the truth."

"Of course not. But I can tell them about Catriona's grave. What happened originally, and this business with the baby. They'll keep it to themselves."

She was with them for over half an hour. I waited in the lounge. Through the window I could see the golf course, green and silent, a carefully tended world utterly remote from the events in which I had become enmeshed. In spite of the wind, small groups of warmly clad golfers were making their way doggedly across the green, driving and putting as though it was the middle of summer.

Harriet returned.

"My car's outside," she said. "I've asked for my case to be brought down."

"I forgot to give you this," I said. I handed her the Hardy.

"What is it?"

"Open it and see."

"I hope my mother-in-law doesn't see you giving me presents."

The string had been tied tightly. Harriet undid it carefully, undoing the knot and rolling up the string as it came free. She pulled off the wrapping and laid it to one side. As she did so, a porter came to the door. I looked round, indicating that we were about to come. When I turned back, I saw Harriet looking at me, her forehead furrowed.

"What is this?" she asked, holding the volume toward me.

"It's a present," I said. "I found it for you on Saturday."

She flung it on the table and stood. She was shaking with anger.

"I don't think this is funny, Andrew. Not one bit. Whatever it is you're playing at, I don't want to know. But if you want my advice, I think you're sick. You don't need me, you need to see a doctor."

She turned and ran to the door. Stunned, I watched her go, unable to make sense of her behavior. Then, looking at the book she had thrown onto the table, I realized that it was bound in dark brown leather. The Hardy had been bound in black. I picked it up, and as I did so felt my heart lurch. It was not possible. I had burned it, burned it and scraped away the ashes.

My hand shook as I lifted the front cover and looked at the title page. The room swayed, and I clutched at the table to steady myself. It was there in black and white, the same title that I had seen all that time ago in the library of the Fraternity of the Old Path:

Kalibool Kolood
aw
Resaalatool Shams ilaal Helaal
sive
Matrix Aeternitatis
aut

Epistola solis ad lunam crescentem
cum versione Latina et notis D. Konigii
And newly Englished by
Nicholas Ockley
Paris, apud Christophorum Beys, Plantini Nepotem
MDXCVIII

With a hand that still trembled, I turned back the page and looked at the flyleaf. There, unchanged, was the same faded and illegible inscription that had been in the copy I had burned.

Chapter

23

I GOT MYSELF BACK TO EDINBURGH on the next bus, scurrying home with my tail between my legs. Harriet's anger had troubled me. Innocent though I knew myself to be, I could not throw off a sense of culpability. For although Duncan Mylne and his associates carried the heaviest blame for the tragic events of the past months, I knew that my own weakness and pride had themselves played no small part in bringing matters to this point.

As the bus raced through the countryside, I sat rigid in my seat, fighting down waves of panic and terror that threatened to overwhelm me. It was all I could do to keep from throwing up. I shivered every time I saw my own reflection in the bus window. A hooded scarecrow made me start. The book nestled in my pocket like a smoking gun. I could not have left it there for Harriet to find if she returned to the lounge. In any case, I knew that any further attempt on my part to destroy or lose it would prove as unsuccessful as the first.

I remembered the words of the old bookseller as he handed it to me, words I had thought a little odd at the time: "This was the book you wanted, wasn't it?" If I had had my wits about me, I would have guessed what he was up to. The first time the book had been left for me to find, in the library, it had, in a sense forced itself on me; I had not taken it home knowingly. When I had found and disposed of it they had been compelled to find a way of tricking me into taking it voluntarily. The old man had asked me if it was the book I wanted, and I had answered that it was. It belonged to me by right.

I knew there was only one way to get rid of it now. Burning it, throwing it in the sea, burying it: none of those would work. The book had to be given back to the old man in person, and he had to be persuaded to take it from me of his own volition, just as I had taken it from him. My only hope of achieving that lay in tricking him in the same way he had tricked me. Whatever evil the book carried in its pages would revert to him, and I would be free of it forever.

The moment I arrived home, I got my boxes of books out of the cupboard. I dumped them on the floor and set aside two which contained spells for protection against evil forces: I thought I might need them before the night was through. They were both volumes that Duncan had loaned me from his own collection.

Sorting through the others, I found one of almost identical dimensions to the *Matrix Aeternitatis*. Carefully removing its cover, I glued it round the older volume. Provided the bookseller did not leaf through it, there was a good chance that he would accept it as a copy of the 1972 reprint of Mathers's edition of the *Key of Solomon*.

I could not possibly carry all my books in one trip, but a mere bagful would be useless as a hiding place for my Trojan horse. The more I could get to the shop in one go, the better.

On my first day at my new address, I had noticed a secondhand bicycle shop a couple of streets away, on Leven Street. I went there now and found just what I needed, an old thing with right-angled handlebars and front and rear baskets, going cheap at ten pounds fifty pence. Back at my flat, I crammed one bag into the rear basket and a second into the front. Dismantling a large cardboard box, I folded it and tied it to the back: once I was at the shop, I would reassemble it and put all the books inside, with the *Matrix* at the bottom.

The bicycle was much too unwieldy to be ridden safely. Perching another box on the saddle, I set off pushing it, making my way back into the maze of side streets. I went unsteadily at first, but by and by settled into the rhythm of pushing and steering. The bicycle had been well oiled and fitted with decent enough tires and brakes.

When I reached the corner of the street off which the shop was situated, I leaned the bike against a wall and set my bags and boxes on the ground. Unfolding my large box, I fixed it together again and began to fill it with books. By the time I had finished, it was immensely heavy.

Leaving the bicycle where it stood, I staggered down the street with the box in both arms. Only then did I wonder what I would do if the shop were closed. With a couple of stops to rest my arms and rebalance my load, I reached the cul-de-sac. I put down the box and looked in both directions. Perhaps I had been mistaken, perhaps this was the wrong street. But on the corner stood the pub that I had noticed on Saturday.

Where the shop had been was just an empty shell. Going closer, I realized that it was indeed the same shop, but utterly changed. It looked as if no one had done business there in years. The sign had been taken down, and over the window only the faintest trace remained of the original name. The door was boarded over, and when I pressed my face against the window I could see nothing but empty shelves and what looked like litter.

Leaving my box outside the shop, I went to the corner and entered the pub. It was almost empty. A woman was cleaning glasses behind the bar. She looked up as I came in, then away again, as if to indicate that customers were not the reason for her being there.

"I'll have a half of Caledonian," I said.

She pulled the half pint without a word and pushed it across the bar. I paid her and took a sip.

"I noticed there's a wee shop round the corner that's empty," I said. "Has it been like that long?"

She looked up, dishcloth in hand, as though making up her mind whether I was human or not.

"You're no from round here, are you?"she said.

"Not far," I answered. "I moved to Drumdryan Street a few weeks ago."

"Student?"

I shook my head.

"I'm looking for work," I said. "Some friends and I were hoping to find a wee place to open a shop. We make leather goods. You know, bags, belts, and stuff."

"Oh, aye?"

She did not seem impressed. Her hand turned listlessly in an empty glass, smearing rather than cleaning it. I took another mouthful of the beer.

"The shop I mentioned would suit us well," I said.

"Where's that?"she asked. She had obviously not noticed my first mention of it.

"Just round the corner. In the cul-de-sac."

"Oh, aye, I know the one you mean. You're wastin' your time."

"Why's that?"

"It hasnae been open in years, not since the old man left. They say no one will take it. Or they'll no rent it out, I'm no sure. It has a bad name."

"I don't understand. What sort of shop was it?"

"I'm told it was a bookshop. This is before my time, you ken. I'm only here five years."

"And what was wrong with it? Did they sell dirty books or something?"

She grimaced and twisted her cloth into a tight roll.

"Do you think a thing like that would worry anyone round here? It wasnae dirty books. It was just . . . I'm told there was something about the old man, something people didnae like. And since he's gone the place has had a bad feeling about it. That's all I know. But no one will take the place. You and your friends would do well to look elsewhere."

I finished my drink and went outside. The box of books was still where I had left it; I had almost hoped that someone might have stolen them. I found the bicycle and brought it round to the cul-de-sac. Looking more closely, I could see that the air of desolation extended beyond the shop, touching in varying degrees the houses on either side of it. Curtainless windows and neglected paintwork suggested that several flats were empty. None of those above the shop seemed occupied.

I was desperate now, sensing that I had been outmaneuvered at every step. It was not yet clear to me why the book should be important, but I associated its presence with a measurable sense of threat. If I could not get rid of it, I would remain in greater danger than ever.

On an impulse, I rifled through the box until I had found the copy of the *Matrix*. Leaving the books against the wall of the shop, I cycled to a corner grocer's shop I had passed on my way. He sold me a small pocket flashlight and batteries. Properly equipped, I went back to find the back alley that served the cul-de-sac. It was a narrow, dingy lane smelling of garbage and dog shit. I found it hard to believe that sunshine ever entered it.

Finding the rear entrance to the shop was a simple matter of counting from the end. There was a rickety gate with a lock that would not have kept a toddler out. A sharp kick and I was in the back-yard.

The door to the shop itself proved more diffi-cult, but a window next to it had been broken. I slipped my hand inside and found a catch. Moments later I was crawling through the open window. Switching on the flashlight, I saw that I was in a tiny room that seemed to have served as a kitchen. There was a sink, and near it an electric ring. Everything was coated in a thick film of dust, as though preserved for the next tenant. A grimy milk bottle stood on the drainboard, there were cans on a shelf, their labels faded and peeling.

I stepped through the open door and found myself in a larger room lined with empty shelves. This must have been where my vanished bookseller kept his better stock. I played the beam of my flash-light along the shelves, wondering if I dared leave the *Matrix Aeternitatis* here. Thinking it over, I knew it would not be enough: he had to take it from me personally.

It was much colder here than it had been out-side. My breath lay on the flashlight's beam like mist. The floor was white with a carpet of undis-turbed dust. The curtain that had been there on my first visit, separating the front of the shop from the rear, still hung in its place, gray and threadbare. No one had been here in a very long time. And I knew that I had made a mistake in coming, that some-thing was very wrong.

It was growing palpable now. What had started as a vague feeling of unease was turning rapidly to a choking sensation and an acute awareness of the presence of real evil. Not only the room in which I stood, not just the shop, but the entire building was saturated with it. I had the sensation that my body had turned to felt. I was limp and immobile, a rag doll equipped with sight and hearing.

As I stood there, perfectly still, struggling for breath and fighting to regain volition, I became aware that a low sound had started in the front of the shop. It was at first impossible to identify it. At one point, I almost thought someone had switched on a radio with the volume turned down. But the sound grew a little at a time until, in a moment of horrified recognition, I realized what it was. Someone was playing a violin, and the piece being played was the adagio from Bach's Violin Sonata in G Minor.

No, not "someone": Catriona. How did I know? Because I had heard her play that piece time and time again until I could anticipate the exact fingering, the pauses, the fractional errors that she always strove to eliminate. Her playing was like a glass with her fingerprints smeared all over it. And I knew there was no recording of her performance, that there never had been.

The playing continued. I remained standing in that same freezing spot, unable to stir, sick at the thought of what might be in the next room, revolted by the thought of what Duncan Mylne had done, terrified by what he planned to do next.

The playing stopped. The last notes lingered on the air for a few moments, then faded and were gone. I was trembling, but still I could not move. The music was still playing in my head, bar after bar like a record. And I knew that, if I closed my eyes I would see Catriona standing with her violin pressed under her chin, her eyes catching mine as she played. I was sick with tension, wondering if it would begin again, the same or another piece. And all the time I knew that the force that held this place together was growing in strength.

I kept my eyes fixed on the curtain separating the front from the rear. The light of the flashlight lay on it, as though it were the curtain in a theater, about to be raised or drawn aside. Each time I breathed, a thin coat of dust settled in my mouth. There was an appalling silence throughout the building.

The curtain rippled suddenly, as though a current of air had passed through it, and then grew still again. I could not move, and I wondered if this was another dream. But even in the most vivid of my dreams I had never felt so frightened. This was real.

I am not sure that I can easily describe what happened next. It still sickens me to think of it. I remained standing in that same spot, expecting at any moment to see Catriona materialize beside me. Had I not just heard her play, had I not seen the curtain move? A moment later, I grew more certain of it: the air around me filled with an unmistakable perfume.

She did not materialize; that is to say, I did not see a figure appear. But out of the darkness I felt something touch my cheek. It was a hand, the skin soft and warm, though I could see nothing. The hand continued to caress my face. I stood there rigid, wanting to scream, to pull away, to run. And then she stepped closer, and her arms were round me, pulling me to her, embracing me. I could feel her body, invisible yet disturbingly real, pressing against me own, and her lips kissing my cheeks, my nose, my forehead, and at last my lips.

It was Catriona, not a simulacrum, not a doppelgänger. I could not mistake the very special physicality of that embrace, the movements of her hands, the teasing and surrender of her lips. I might almost have succumbed, might have given in to the embrace and put my own arms round her: dear God, I came so very close to that. My reason screamed at me to run, my eyes told me there was nothing there, that, whatever it was, it was not Catriona; but my body, so unexpectedly caressed, had its own responses.

It came to me that I had once read in one of the books lent me by Duncan that if a succubus came to a man, whether waking or in a dream, he should turn to it and ask its name. I pulled my lips away from the mouth that was kissing mine.

"What is your name?" I asked. And then in Latin and Hebrew and Arabic, "What is your name?"

The air that had been so sweetly perfumed changed suddenly, and I started coughing as though ashes, newly burned, had been pressed against my face. Instead of lips against my face, I felt a tongue licking my skin; not a human tongue, but longer and rough to the touch.

Whether it was my sudden revulsion or the mere effect of the question I had asked, I found myself capable of movement. I turned and ran for the door. Behind me, a voice started calling. Catriona's voice.

"Andrew, come back. It's me, I need you, Andrew . . . "

I carried on running and did not stop until I had reached the alleyway. My bicycle was waiting where I had left it.

Chapter 24

THE *MATRIX AETERNITATIS* WAS still in my coat pocket. There was no point in going back for the other books: the old man would stay out of my way to be sure he gave me no opportunity to palm the volume back on to him.

I sat alone for a long time, trying to regain my composure. My nerves were in shreds, and even though I downed three or four glasses of whisky in a row, I could not calm myself. It may sound trivial to write of it, but to be embraced so materially by what was less than air had filled me with a sense of loathing as though, making love to a beautiful young woman, I had opened my eyes to find myself bedded with a bare corpse.

Since I could not now rid myself of that hateful book, I decided to look at it more closely and to see if I could determine why it had been forced on me and why its presence seemed to bring such horrors in its wake. I got up and took the copy from my pocket.

I could see straightaway that it possessed two titles. The first, *Kalibool Kolood*, meant "The Matrix of Eternal Life." The second title, *Resaalatool Shams ilaal Helaal* meant "The Epistle of the Sun to the New Moon."

I reread the short prologue by the English translator, Nicholas Ockley, but nothing in it shed any light on my dilemma. Ockley did not, in fact, seem to know much about either the book or its author beyond their evil reputation, and, as I read his translation, it gradually became apparent to me that he had worked, not from the original Arabic, but from the Latin, and that the Latin itself was by no means always faithful to the original.

Confused by these misreadings and the uncertainty they provoked in me, I determined to try my hand at the original. I still had my dictionaries and grammars, and I thought I could make good progress with what help the translations might provide.

I discovered two things straightaway: the author's identity and the period when he had lived. Both the Latinizer and Ockley called him Avimetus, but in the exordium to the Arabic version the author had written out his name in full, together with that of his father, as was the custom: "*wa min ba'd. Hakadha yaqul al-'abd al-fani* . . . To begin: Thus says this evanescent servant, Abu Ahmad 'Abd Allah ibn Sulayman al-Fasi al-

Maghribi. . . . " Abu Ahmad 'Abd Allah, the son of Solomon, the man from Fez, the Moroccan . . .

I set the book down. A horrid truth had started to dawn. Of course, I could very well have guessed the first part of his name from the Latin form: Avimetus would have come from the old spelling, Aboo Ahmet, thus Avoo Ahmetus, thus Avimetus. But the rest would have meant nothing even had I read them that first time. Now, however . . .

I leafed to the back of the *Fara'id*, the dictionary of classical Arabic I had used while in Morocco. During my sessions with Sheikh Ahmad, I had sometimes jotted down notes on the blank pages at the back. In the course of one lesson, he had explained to me something of his lineage. I had written the details down dutifully, without giving them real attention. Now I looked more closely.

He was, he had said, born Ahmad, the son of 'Abd Allah. That meant that his father would have been called Abu Ahmad 'Abd Allah—"the father of Ahmad, 'Abd Allah." I looked at my notes again. Ahmad's grandfather had been called Sulayman, his great-grandfather 'Abd al-Rasul, and his great-great-grandfather 'Umar.

I picked up the *Matrix* again and leafed through the first few pages. There on the third page was what I was looking for: "I learned these things from my father, who learned them in turn from his father Sulayman; and Sulayman had them from his father 'Abd al-Rasul, who had them from his father 'Umar."

It did not seem possible that this, a book whose English translation had been published in

1598, could have been written by the father of a man I had spoken to only a few months earlier. But Duncan Mylne's voice echoed repeatedly through my head: *In the account he left of their meeting, he wrote that the sheikh was already an old man then.*

But when had the author of the *Matrix* himself lived? I turned at once to the colophon, a brief passage at the end of a text where the author would give brief details of the date when he had completed his task, or the scribe the day he ended the labor of transcription. I was not disappointed. Sheikh Abu Ahmad had followed convention to the letter:

"Completed by the hand of this wretched servant in the imperial city of Fez on the fifth day of Rabi' al-Awwal 585, in the reign of the just and benevolent Caliph, Lord of Spain and Morocco, Sultan Ya'qub ibn Yusuf al-Mansur."

It could not have been clearer. The *Kalibool Kolood* had been finished on the twenty-third of April 1189.

The purpose of the letter was not hard to find. In it, Abu Ahmad claimed, he had passed on to his eldest son the secret of all secrets, the key to mastery over life and death. Anyone who wished to conquer death should recite the spells and perform the rituals detailed in the text.

The purpose of the *Matrix Aeternitatis*, then, was to teach men a method for attaining everlasting life, not through religion or mysticism or alchemy, but by magic. The book itself was to be the matrix for survival. But by the time I had finished reading, I was certain that there was something more to it than that, and I was reasonably certain what it was: the power to return to life those already dead.

Chapter

25

IT WAS DARK, and I was frightened. I had not realized until now quite how ancient was the evil that had been wrapping me in its cloak for so many months. I thought of d'Hervilly in his cold mansion above Tangier, paying homage to gods older than the city. Of faces glimpsed by fire- or candlelight, old faces, heavily wrinkled, with the scent of death on them. And that terrible old man in Fez, sleeping death's sleep each night, veiled like the new moon in darkness, ready to rise and grow again. Sheikh Abu Ahmad had promised eternal life: but what sort of life, and on what conditions?

I could not bear to stay in my flat. Remembering my promise to ring my mother every night, I went out to the phone box. My mother answered straightaway; she sounded more worried than before.

"He had another attack today. It's still with him, poor soul; he's in terrible pain. The doctor say he's to be flown ashore as soon as possible. They've reserved a bed for him at the Royal Northern Infirmary in Inverness. I'll be going with him, of course. No doubt if he needs to go to Edinburgh they'll send him there. Do you think you could manage to come up?"

I hesitated. There was no real excuse I could give, and I could not begin to tell my mother the true reason.

"I'll do what I can," I said. "Give me a day or two to clear things here."

"He'll not be in that long, Andrew. He's only to be in a couple of days, just for them to run their tests. A scan of some sort, the doctor said he'd have."

"I'm sure that's right, though I daresay they'll find nothing. No tumor or anything like that."

"You sound very certain, Andrew. I wish I could be as sure as you. Even Dr. Boyd says he doesn't know what they'll find."

"Let's say it's an instinct I have."

"Do come up, son. He'll be pleased to see you, I know. He'll only speak in Gaelic now. Every night he has bad dreams, but he won't say what they're about. Maybe he'll talk to you. It would do him good."

We talked a little longer, and I promised I would ring the following night. I said nothing about Catriona's grave or the dead child found there. If my mother had read the newspaper reports, she would not have guessed the identity of the grave, and it was better for her to remain in ignorance.

When I put down the receiver, I saw that it had grown even darker outside. It was late now, and the pubs were either closing or closed. I had nowhere to go except back to my rooms. The thought curdled inside me like sour milk. I picked up the phone again and asked for information. They gave me the number of Harriet's hotel. I rang reception and asked to be put through.

"Yes, who is it?"

"It's me. Andrew. Please don't put down the phone. I have to speak to you. I wasn't to blame for what happened this morning."

There was a long pause. I expected her to slam the receiver down any moment, but she did not. Finally, she broke the silence.

"I'm sorry about what happened this morning, Andrew. It was rude of me. But—"

"You didn't stay, you didn't give me a chance to explain."

"I'm sorry, but after—"

"You treated me like someone who would deliberately play a trick like that on you. Didn't you think about it afterward? Didn't you ask yourself why I would want to do a thing like that?"

"I thought maybe you . . . I don't know. That you were sick . . . "

Her voice tailed away. She did not want to be more explicit.

"The book was put there in place of a copy of *Desperate Remedies*. I bought it for you in a shop off Leith Walk yesterday afternoon. It cost me four pounds. The bookseller substituted the book you saw for the one I bought. Do you believe me?"

"I . . . Andrew, I just don't know. The whole thing seems so incredible."

"It is incredible. I can't take it in any more than you. But it is happening. Iain is dead. My father has started to have the same symptoms. Catriona's grave has been tampered with twice, and a child has been killed. Do you believe any of those things?"

"Of course I do, but—"

"Then believe me when I tell you I did not know that book was in the package. If you're willing to listen to me, I can tell you more about the book and why it was placed there."

There was a short pause.

"Very well," she said, "I'll come in the morning."

"No, tonight."

"Andrew . . . "

"Please, Harriet. Tomorrow may be too late. I can't take the risk of falling asleep on my own. He's close, I know he is."

"What is it, Andrew? What are your frightened of?"

"Mylne, don't you see? He's looking for me. He's getting desperate. He needs me to bring back Catriona from the dead. It's what he chose me for, why he trained me, why he revealed so many of his secrets to me. Come tonight, Harriet. It may be too late in the morning."

There was a long pause.

"All right," she said. Her voice sounded very far away. "I'll need your address."

*　　*　　*

THE STREETS WERE ABNORMALLY QUIET. I walked back past tall gray buildings, pursued by echoes. My footsteps were magnified. Once, I thought I heard scurrying at my back, but when I looked round the pavement was empty.

I let myself in and made my way upstairs nervously. My neighbors on the first two floors had gone away for the weekend and would not be back till morning. The house, like the streets outside, was dark and silent. Nothing moved. Yet.

Locking my door, I took out the two books I had kept back and found the passages I needed. Starting with the lintel above my door, I began to construct a series of magical defences against the forces threatening me. I drew pentacles and circles that I filled with spells and symbolic devices. It was, I knew, the work of a novice, but I had nothing else with which to ward off any attack.

Shortly after midnight, my doorbell rang. Harriet had not wasted any time. As I let her in, I saw her look askance at the circles and stars with which I had covered my door and the middle of the floor.

"Believe me," I said, "they are necessary."

"They look like the work of a madman, Andrew. And look at you, you're in a dreadful state. You haven't shaved, you probably haven't eaten."

"That isn't important."

"Yes," she said impatiently, "it is. If you let yourself go, you'll just become weaker. I still don't understand what this is all about, but I'm sure most of it has to do with mental states. Come on, get yourself tidied up while I make us something to eat."

"There's nothing in the kitchen."

"You don't imagine I hadn't thought of that? I stopped and got some things on the way. Now hurry up, you're making me nervous."

I showered, shaved, and washed my hair. In the bedroom I found fresh underwear and a shirt. I felt fresher than I had done in days. Harriet had made a curry, and it was already on the table. I sat down opposite her, cheered by her presence, feeling hope return, and with it sudden appetite.

"I feel as if I haven't eaten in days," I said.

"You probably haven't had a decent meal in months. This isn't up to much, but what can you expect a girl to find on a Sunday night on the outskirts of Edinburgh?"

We ate in silence for a while. Slowly, a sense of harmony was restored between us. I began to tell Harriet what I knew about the *Matrix* and she listened without interrupting, with great attentiveness. When I finished, she sat for a while deep in thought, toying with the last of her rice.

"You must not go to see your father," she said at last.

"I know, but I need to talk to him. He can help me, I know he can."

She shook her head.

"If Mylne had Iain killed in order to stop him warning you about him, he won't stop at killing your father."

"You believe me, then?" I asked.

"Your father's symptoms are really the same as Iain's?"

I nodded.

"Identical, as far as I can tell. It's too much of a coincidence."

"Yes, it is. But I don't understand how Mylne knew your father was planning to come here. And I don't know why I haven't been attacked myself."

"I've wondered about that too," I said, "but I don't have an answer."

"You said you thought Mylne wanted to bring Catriona back to life."

"Yes, I do. That's why he had her body dug up. That's the reason for the objects found in the grave, the dead child. It's all there in the *Matrix Aeternitatis*. You can read it for yourself later. Even in the English translation it's quite clear."

"Why do you suppose he needs you?"

"That's in the book as well. The seventh chapter. If the ritual is performed by someone to whom the dead person had a close attachment, someone they want to return to and who would desire to have them back, there is a much higher chance of success."

"It's not automatic, then?"

I shook my head.

"There are serious dangers, both physical and spiritual, but mainly the latter. The smallest error in any of the rituals can result in tragedy. There have been cases of the wrong person being brought back. Of forces being incarnated that have outgrown the magician's control. Things have entered this world from outside that should never have been allowed in. I can't make sense of everything he writes, but the sense of danger is very immediate. If Mylne could persuade me to perform the necessary rites, Catriona's return would be that much more certain."

"But why does he want her at all?"

"I'm not entirely sure. To question her, I think. She has knowledge he craves."

"Isn't she back already? You said you smelled her perfume yesterday morning."

"That isn't all," I said. I explained what had happened earlier that day in the shop.

"It was Catriona," I said. "Only she could have played the violin exactly like that. And it was her voice I heard. But what I felt later . . . That was not my wife, it was something else using her. I don't really understand this, it's too complicated for me. I think Mylne has been able to bring her back in part, but not all the way. He needs more, much more. But if he gets it wrong . . . "

WE FINISHED OUR MEAL and washed up. I gave Harriet my bed and made myself comfortable on the couch. She asked for the copy of the *Matrix Aeternitatis* to read, and I gave it to her, first making sure that the page with the woodcut had been sealed with paper-clips.

"I'm glad my parents-in-law aren't here," she said. "They'd have a fit."

"Were they very upset earlier?"

"Yes. They don't know what's going on. I've told them you're a friend of Iain's, and that you're in trouble."

"You didn't say what sort of trouble, did you?"

"What do you think?"

I smiled.

"Thanks for agreeing to come. I couldn't have gone through another night alone."

"Will anything happen now that I'm here?"

"I don't know. But I think we should both try to get some sleep."

I was desperately tired. Alone, I could not have slept, but knowing that Harriet was in the next room gave me confidence. As soon as she had gone to bed, I switched off the light and fell asleep almost at once.

I was woken by a soft light playing across my eyes. I lifted a hand to shield them and saw nothing behind the light but darkness.

"Andrew."

It was Harriet's voice, soft but urgent, bringing me fully awake.

"Andrew, wake up."

I could see her now, standing in the open doorway of the bedroom. She was dressed in a long gown that reached to her ankles. Her hair was tossed.

I lifted myself against the arm of the couch and swung my legs onto the floor, dislodging the quilt beneath which I had been lying. Harriet came into the living room.

"What is it?" I asked. She looked scared.

"It's starting, Andrew. I can hear something upstairs. It began a couple of minutes ago."

At first there was nothing: just the same stillness in which I had been sleeping. Then I heard it too. Flapping and scraping, flapping and scraping, and at times the dull thumping of things like feet.

Harriet joined me on the couch. We sat side by side, listening as the sounds moved across the floor upstairs and reached the door to the attic. There was the sound of a door opening, then a muffled shuffling on the stairs.

"Can it get in?" asked Harriet.

"I don't know," I said. It had never approached this close before. We listened as it came down the attic stairs, then came flapping along the landing. It stopped as it reached the door of my flat.

There was a long silence, then something began to move bodily against the door, flapping to and fro like an eyeless, sightless creature that can smell what it is looking for. Harriet clung to me. I could do nothing more than what I had done. If the circles I had drawn did not protect us, we were defenceless against whatever it was.

And then, more horrifying than any of the other sounds, a voice spoke from the other side of the door.

"Andrew, open the door. Please open the door, Andrew."

I froze. The voice was Catriona's. Not a simulacrum, but her real voice, in every measure.

"Please, Andrew. It's cold out here. Please let me in."

"What is it?" Harriet asked. "Who is it?"

"It's Catriona," I said.

I stood up. Harriet grabbed my wrist, trying to pull me back to the couch.

"For God's sake, don't go to her, Andrew. It isn't real. She isn't there. Catriona's dead."

I pulled my hand free.

"I know she's dead. That's why I have to keep her out."

I found one of the two books I had used for my defensive spells and flicked through it quickly. It contained a conjuration against evil from *Picatrix*, an infamous Arabic work of sorcery dating from the tenth century and falsely ascribed to the Moorish scholar al-Majriti. I found the verses I wanted and, standing at the door, recited them slowly.

The pleading voice changed in seconds. There was a loud scream, then sobbing, then a deeper voice commanding me to open the door. I went on reading, though my voice shook and I felt sick with fear.

When I came to the end, the voice had lost some of its strength, but none of its anger. I rejoined Harriet on the couch. At the door, something started to scrabble and lick at the wood.

"Let me in, Andrew," came Catriona's voice again. I did not answer. Losing patience, she threw herself at the door, howling. Still I did not answer.

It went on like that until dawn. I read and reread the conjuration until I knew it by heart. Harriet and I sat huddled together in that cold room, while my dead wife howled and scrabbled at the door. Until that night, I had feared death only as a great darkness and an oblivion. Now it is not oblivion I fear: it is oblivion I pray for every night.

Chapter 26

WITH DAWN CAME PEACE. We remained on the couch like lovers, held together by fear rather than passion. The silence continued, strengthening with the light, and bit by bit we fell asleep.

I dreamed it was still night and I was in the dark cathedral again. The white-robed congregation had gone, and I sensed that I was alone in the vast building. Alone, and yet not alone. On my right, I could make out a row of tombs, not unlike those depicted in the woodcut in the *Matrix*. Beside them, a door lay open. Behind it, dark stairs led down to a crypt. And on the stairs I could hear the sound of something moving very slowly.

It was late when I finally awoke. Harriet had got up a little before me and was busy in the kitchen preparing breakfast. There was nothing to eat but toast and coffee, with a few eggs Harriet had bought the night before.

"It wasn't a dream, was it?" she asked.

I shook my head.

"I'm sorry for you," she said. "To have her there all night. It must have been . . . "

"I just keep telling myself it wasn't really Catriona. But it makes little difference. The voice is hers. If I'd opened the door . . . Well, I wonder what I might have seen." I paused. My limbs felt dull and heavy, my head ached. "I want her to be at rest again. Out of his reach, out of all their reach."

"Don't you want to have her back? If it could be done. Not that thing, but Catriona."

"Would you have Iain back?"

She did not answer right away. Her eyes remained fixed on a point just behind me, unmoving, while she imagined what it would be like to see him again, to be able to wipe out death unconditionally as if it had been nothing more than an indelicate stain.

"Yes," she said at last. "I don't think I would care what it cost. I wake up every night wanting him so much . . . "

I looked at her gently, understanding. There were tears in her eyes. What right had I to disabuse her of whatever little hope she might be building for herself?

"Even if it was not the Iain you used to know?"

"You said Catriona was not a simulacrum, that she was real. Her voice, the music, the perfume—all real."

"There is more than one reality, Harriet."

"I suppose Mylne taught you that."

"Yes, he did. Do you deny it on that account?"

She shook her head.

"Of course not. It just sounds so trite. It may be true, but not for me. This is the only reality I've ever known or am likely to know. If Iain were here with me, if I could see and hear and touch him, he would be part of this reality, my reality."

"Then you would be wrong. What you would see would be something else, something born from a different matrix. It would never be Iain, any more than that thing outside the door last night was Catriona."

She shuddered and stood up.

"Well, there's no point in speculating, is there? Iain isn't going to come back. We have to concentrate on the matter at hand."

"Which is?"

"Forcing Mylne to stop. We need to enlist some help. Some of Iain's colleagues at New College used to take this sort of thing seriously. You know some of them yourself."

"Yes, but they probably know less about these matters than I do."

"We have to start somewhere. They may know of someone more knowledgeable. Will you come with me?"

"If you like."

I packed the *Matrix Aeternitatis* in my briefcase, along with the two books I had used for my protection the night before. At least Harriet would lend my story some backing. But I was by no means sure we were doing the right thing.

I opened the door. Though there had been no sounds for several hours now, it was with the greatest trepidation that we stepped out onto the landing. As I turned to shut the door behind me, I noticed that the wood was gouged with deep scratches, as though someone had been ripping at it with an awl. Or with naked claws. Harriet had not noticed, and I did not draw it to her attention.

WE WALKED INTO TOWN. More than anything, we needed fresh air on our faces, the touch of sunshine, a sense of normality. By the time we reached the top of Johnston Terrace, the events of the night had indeed taken on the appearance of a dream. Had it not been that we both remembered each and every incident with the selfsame clarity, I think I might very well have pretended to myself that nothing was amiss after all.

We walked down past the castle to the Lawnmarket, then turned left on Bank Street, heading for the Mound. As we did so, Harriet stopped.

"Andrew, would you mind if I drop in at my solicitor's? His office isn't far from here. I should have thought of it before, when I knew we were coming this way. He has some papers for me to sign. I was going to call in next week, but now I'm here I may as well get it over with."

It was an old family firm above a clothing store in Cockburn Street. The partner who dealt with Harriet's affairs, a Mr. Merchiston, was just finishing with a client: would we mind waiting for a few minutes?

Coffee was brought to a waiting room for us. We sat watching fish swim in a long, coral-filled tank. A purple fire-fish hung before the glass, gazing at a world it could not comprehend, a different reality upon which, without knowing it, it was wholly dependent.

My father had kept tropical fish, thinking it a special challenge to possess on a cold northern island creatures from the warm waters of the Pacific or the Caribbean. In my teens, I had helped him look after the tanks, learning the rituals of feeding, changing water, and testing the various chemical balances.

"The tiniest change will kill them," I said. "Too much salt, too little salt, too many nitrites, a few degrees' rise in temperature, a few degrees' fall . . . "

"A little like us," said Harriet.

"In a way. It's what Mylne tried to teach me, that the smallest change in a ritual could produce incalculable effects. A word misplaced, a gesture inexpertly performed, the correct performance at the wrong time—any one of them could have unwanted consequences. Nothing could be left to chance."

A mandarin goby hung against a piece of white coral, feeding slowly, oblivious of the narrow limits within which it lived. It rose briefly to the surface, then fell and vanished behind a rock.

A man came through the door of the waiting room, his hand extended.

"Harriet, how nice to see you. I didn't expect you so soon. How have you been?"

He was in his forties, neatly dressed, balding in

front, a sober man in a quiet suit, well accustomed to the coming and going of widows. Round spectacles framed in gold caught a double image of fish swimming in the tank. Yet another reality. I wondered if the fish could see themselves reflected there; did they think, perhaps, there was another world than their tank, that they would swim there after death?

"I'm fine," replied Harriet. "It was hard at the start of term, but I got used to it. You were right, it was good to go back to work."

"I thought it was half term."

"It is. I decided to stay in Edinburgh after all. And since I was passing, I thought I'd drop in and sign those papers. Oh, I'm sorry, I'm being rude. This is a friend of mine, Dr. Macleod. He was a colleague of Iain's."

Merchiston stuck out a hand.

"Pleased to meet you. I won't keep Mrs. Gillespie long. There are just a few formalities."

He ushered her to the door, then, as he started to follow her, turned back to me.

"Macleod?" he said. "Not Andrew Macleod by any chance?"

"Yes, that's right."

"Well, this is a stroke of luck. I've been trying to get hold of you. I sent a letter to you at New College a little while ago, but it mustn't have reached you."

"Not at New College," I said. "I was attached to the university."

"Oh, I'm sorry, I must have misunderstood. Harriet said you were a colleague of Iain's."

"Yes, but not in the same institution. I took some seminars for him, that's all."

"Well, it's a good thing you called in, then. If you'll wait just a moment, I have something for you."

He and Harriet disappeared, and I was left wondering what was going on. He returned in a couple of minutes bearing a small envelope.

"Iain gave this to me before he died," he said. "I had instructions to give it to you as soon as you returned from Algeria."

"Morocco," I said. "I was in Morocco."

"Yes, of course. Naturally, there was no way to contact you there. If you could just scribble your signature on this form, you can take the packet with you."

I signed on the spot he indicated and he passed the envelope to me.

"Did Iain say what this is?" I asked.

He shook his head.

"Just that it was important to get it to you. He was insistent about that. It seemed to worry him."

"I think I know what it is. Will Harriet be long?"

"Ten minutes or so. There are some things I have to explain to her."

He left, and I sat down again, clutching the envelope to me. I decided to wait until Harriet returned. I did not want to read Iain's letter alone.

THE ACANTHUS IS A CAFÉ near the station that serves light lunches. We both needed strong coffee and a place to sit and read. While we waited to be served, I tore open the envelope. Inside was a short hand-written letter. Judging by the writing, Iain had penned the letter in more than one session. His hand clearly betrayed the stages of his physical deterioration, growing increasingly illegible as it neared the end. I read it slowly, then passed it to Harriet without comment. There was nothing I needed to add.

Chapter 27

Dear Andrew, the letter began, *I'm sorry we didn't have longer to talk when we last met. I know a bit more now about the pressures you've been under lately, and I apologize for my clumsy attempt to put you right. Please put it down to inexperience, and the fact that I was concerned for you. I know I should have been more tactful, but you were my friend, and I wanted to help you. I suppose it goes with the job and the collar. Still, I should have known better, and I do apologize.*

All the same I have to say I'm more certain than I ever was that I was right to warn you against Duncan Mylne. Perhaps you'll have seen enough by now to convince you he means you harm; if not, I suppose you've already have torn up this letter.

I said I'd heard rumors about Mylne, that he had an evil reputation in some quarters; but I didn't know then just how evil that reputation was, or how well merited. The things I heard in the beginning encouraged me to find out more. It wasn't easy. Even in the church, people I asked about him would say a little and then clam up. That just made me more determined to see what lay behind all the secrecy.

I got my breakthrough a few days before that last visit to your flat. That was the real reason why I called, to tell you what I already knew and what I planned to do next; but when Mylne turned up I couldn't risk staying. I meant to get in touch with you after that, and I would have done, if it hadn't been for this illness.

You may have heard me speak of Angus Brodie, a member of the General Assembly and a good friend of mine. Sometimes he's called in by people who've been troubled by . . . let's say, evil spirits. Angus doesn't call what he does exorcism, since our church does not recognize the practice; but there are cases now and again when something more than simple prayers are needed.

I mentioned Mylne to him, and he told me what he knew, which was more or less the same as I'd heard from other people. But he then said that, in more serious cases, he was assisted by a friend, a Catholic priest. As you can imagine, this is not something he'd like

known to all and sundry, least of all his more
puritan colleagues on the Assembly. All the
same, he was good enough to give me the
priest's name, and I made an appointment to
see him.

The writing broke off here, and when it
resumed was in a different ink and a much altered
hand.

I've been very ill these past few days. The
headaches get more and more intense until I
think my head will crack open. I don't know
how much longer I can bear them. The doc-
tors say they can find nothing wrong. That
doesn't surprise me. I know very well what's
responsible for my sickness. It won't show up
in any tests.

Between bouts I feel weak but clear-
headed. Harriet tells me you've gone to
Morocco with Mylne, and I'm afraid he has
you for good now. But I still feel I should
write this in the very small hope it may do
good, and because I know I do not have long.
I'll be dead before you return, Andrew, I
know that.

I wouldn't mind so much, were it not for
the dreams I've been having. Have you been
dreaming too? I suspect you have. There is a
hooded figure that troubles me greatly.
Sometimes he appears in the daytime, when
I'm awake. For moments only, then he's
gone. I've been seeing more of him lately,

*when the pain is bad. Once he sat on the edge
of my bed for over an hour, just watching me.
I'm terrified that he will lift his hood and that
I shall see his face.*

*I visited the priest two days after I saw
you, and came away more shaken than I have
ever been. His name is Father Silvestri, and
he lives alone in a small parish house in
Corstorphine. He was cautious at first, even
though I'd brought a letter of introduction
from Angus. But when I told him why I'd
come and what I knew already, he agreed to
help.*

*Andrew, you must go to Silvestri as soon
as you read this. Go without delay: he will tell
you everything. Listen to what he says and
follow whatever instructions he may give you.
And make sure you get away from Mylne,
whatever the cost. Silvestri told me things
almost past belief. He told me all he knew
about Mylne, and he showed me proof to back
it up. Silvestri is not a madman, and I believe
every word he said. Duncan Mylne is not
what he seems. He is not even human in any
real sense of the word. You must believe me.
He . . .*

The writing broke off again, and when it
resumed it was clear that Iain's condition had dete-
riorated markedly in the meantime.

*Have to finish or this thing will never
end. Harriet must not know. So hard to leave*

her alone. Look after her, Andrew. Silvestri has been, but he can do nothing. We pray, but our prayers are not strong enough against that man.

Have you seen the church, Andrew? You know the one I mean, you must know. The gray church It's in my dreams every night now, sometimes I think I shall go mad, for I believe I shall wake up there. Dear God, the sounds I hear

The writing trailed off again. At the very end, Iain had scribbled a few lines, broken and barely legible. I read them with great difficulty. They were the last words he ever wrote.

Find the church. Destroy everything They are swarming Angus Mylne brought them back from Morocco

Chapter 28

HARRIET SET DOWN THE LETTER. I watched her, saying nothing, knowing it was not yet time to speak. I could see that she was fighting hard to keep control of her emotions. She had just read her husband's last written words, only to find them the ravings of a frightened man suffering from delusions. That is how it must have seemed to her.

So we sat like that for fifteen minutes, the silence between us tight and uninterrupted by the noises around us, until Harriet was calm once more, and ready to discuss whatever consequences might follow from Iain's account.

"He came to the house," she said at last.

I looked at her in horror.

"No, not Mylne," she said, correctly interpreting my expression. "The priest, Father Silvestri. He came two or three times before Iain died. They spent about an hour together each time. I asked Iain about him, of course, but he would never explain. I assumed Silvestri was someone he had worked with. Iain used to be quite involved with ecumenical matters, and I knew he'd made close friends with several priests. He came to the funeral as well. I saw him in the distance, but he never spoke to me."

"Silvestri must have been trying to save Iain from Mylne," I said.

"It didn't do much good, did it?"

I looked at her. Her hands were flat on the table, the fingers close together, the nails filed hard down.

"It depends on what you mean," I said. "We don't know what Silvestri was trying to save him from. Death may have been the least of Iain's fears."

She lifted her hands and smoothed her hair back. Today she wore it tied behind, a little severely. Her forehead was smooth and white, her eyebrows dark against the skin. I both pitied and feared her.

"This thing about a church," she said. "Does that mean anything to you?"

I nodded.

"Yes, I think so."

"He used to talk about it a lot in the days before he died. A dark church with a veil across the chancel. We thought he was just raving. He was incoherent, seldom in his right mind."

"Oh, he knew what he was talking about," I said. "There is a church."

"You know where it is?"

I nodded.

"And you know what's inside it, what it is you're supposed to destroy?"

I nodded again. Through a window to my left I could see cars and buses slip past, people walking, trees shedding their leaves—a world over which I had once thought to obtain mastery. *Destroy everything They are swarming*

"We'll speak to Silvestri before we do anything," she said.

I was finding it hard to concentrate. The thought of entering the church again filled me with dread. *They are swarming*

"You're right," I said. "But, as you said, he couldn't save Iain, and I don't suppose he can do any more for us."

"Do you have any better suggestions?"

"I'm worried about my father," I said.

"Silvestri . . ."

I shook my head.

"No, he can't help. Maybe . . . I've been thinking that I should take Iain's letter to Ramsey McLean. He's a close friend of my father's, he'll want to help. And he is a doctor, he may understand what's wrong."

"He won't believe a word of that letter."

"But he may see some sort of connection. I have to try."

I FOUND A TELEPHONE KIOSK and rang McLean's surgery. His reception said he had just returned from his morning rounds, and that he was about to have lunch. I gave my name, and a few moments later I was put through.

"Dr. McLean? This is Andrew Macleod."

"Andrew? Goodness, it's been some time since I last saw you. I thought you'd left town."

"My job here finished, but I decided to stay on. Listen, I need to speak with you urgently."

"Is this on a medical matter?"

I hesitated.

"Not exactly," I said. "But indirectly. My father is very ill."

"I'm sorry to hear that. What's the matter with him?"

"It's hard to explain," I said. "Is there any chance you can see me today? I'd like a bit longer than the usual consultation."

"Come at four," he said. "I can get one of my colleagues to fill in."

"Are you sure that's all right?"

"Of course. If your father's ill, I want to do what I can to help. I'll be waiting for you at four o'clock."

A TAXI LEFT US AT SILVESTRI'S DOOR. We had been given the address by the Catholic diocesan office. It was an unpretentious house next door to a church and facing a religious primary school. A housekeeper opened the door and we gave our names. She asked us to wait in a little room off the hall, a brown-painted room with a shabby carpet and straight-backed chairs. The walls were decorated with religious pictures of the dully pious variety. An air of solemnity hung over everything. There was a very great silence throughout the house, and the raised hands of the saints in their black frames seemed to warn against speech or laughter.

Several minutes passed. We glanced self-consciously at one another from time to time, neither one daring to say a word, as though we were children in school awaiting a teacher's discipline. Finally, the door opened. An old man in a loose black suit and dog collar stood facing us.

"I am Silvestri," he said. "What can I do for you?"

Harriet got to her feet. She seemed ill at ease.

"We've met once or twice before," she said. "You came to my house to visit my husband Iain when he was ill. And I saw you at his funeral."

"Iain Gillespie," the priest said. "Yes, I remember him. I am so sorry. He was very young."

Harriet nodded, but did not pursue the subject of Iain's death. She turned to me, then back to Silvestri.

"This is Andrew Macleod. I'm sure you know his name. Iain told you about him, told you he was afraid Andrew was in danger from a man called Mylne."

I saw the look in the old man's eyes. Not fear, but something very like it, something more terrible. He was a thin, academic-looking man of around seventy, a Jesuit, one of those desiccated priests with a scrawny neck protruding from his collar like a plant out of a pot, but not a bit funny. There was something grim and old-fashioned about him, an air of suffering and knowledge. The skin tight to the bone, the flesh wasted, the heart and the mind burned for the sake of faith.

"You have broken from Mylne?" he asked. His jaw was tense. He did not once take his eyes from me.

I nodded.

"But he won't give me up," I said. "Things have been happening. I . . . can't go on."

He did not close his eyes, but I sensed him close himself off, as though drawing a curtain about his person, or an invisible shield.

"Iain has told us about his meetings with you," said Harriet. "He left details in a letter."

"Then you know all there is to know."

Harriet shook her head vigorously.

"No," she said, "we know next to nothing. Only rumor and innuendo, things we can't hold on to. Iain said you would tell us the rest, that you would help us."

"I can't help anyone," said the priest. "If you've become entangled with Mylne, you're beyond my reach. I can pray for you, but nothing more."

Harriet held out Iain's letter, which she had taken from her bag.

"Please," she said. "Read the letter."

Silvestri hesitated. He seemed arthritic, but held himself erect against whatever pain there was.

"It's too late," he said. "If you had come to me sooner, when you first met Mylne, perhaps . . . "

"Please," I said. "We have no one else to turn to."

The hesitation again, then the most impercepti-ble of nods. He held out his hand. Harriet handed him the letter, unfolded. He took a pair of pince-nez from his breast pocket and slipped them on his nose. He read carefully, without remark. Once or twice, I saw his face tighten. But his hands were steady. They were the steadiest hands I think I have ever seen. As though he were laced with iron. When he reached the end, he folded the letter and passed it back to Harriet.

"Thank you," he said. "Your husband is still remembered in my prayers, every night and every morning."

He seemed to be making up his mind about something. But where most men would have looked at the carpet or through the window, he kept his eyes fixed on me. I felt he could see into me.

"You had better tell me what you know," he said. "And what has happened between you and Mylne. This is not a comfortable room. Come with me."

He led us to a larger room, a sparsely furnished sitting room where, I imagine, he saw his parishioners or held conversations with his fellow priests. A red light burned steadily in front of a sacred picture. On one wall, a wooden crucifix hung heavily from a brass hook.

"Where shall I begin?" I asked.

"At the beginning."

Chapter

29

WHEN I CAME TO A HALT, Silvestri said nothing, but got up and crossed to a cupboard. He brought back a plain wooden box, a container for sacred wafers.

"These are not as yet consecrated," he said, lifting the lid. "But in due course they will be. During the mass, they will undergo a process known as transubstantiation. I am sure you are familiar with the term. They will be transformed into the body of Christ. While retaining the appearance and taste and smell of bread, they will become flesh in substance.

"Your friend, Iain, of course, did not believe that the host actually becomes flesh. For him it was a spiritual process, a symbol, nothing more tangible. And for you, I expect it means even less. It is merely a charade, a performance put on for the gullible.

"That is why Duncan Mylne was so hard for Iain to understand, and why it was so easy for him to win you over. Iain, because he believed in the spirit, but not the flesh; you, because you believed only in the flesh."

He looked at Harriet.

"My church has never abandoned the miraculous. We still have our saints, our relics, our moving statues, our bleeding images. In doing away with all that, your husband closed his eyes to the magic inherent in faith. I do not blame him. There have been serious abuses on account of miracles. Dr. Macleod is right to think that the gullible are sometimes cheated. But there is more depth in the miraculous than you may think."

He paused, then turned back to me.

"Whenever I perform the mass, am I not a little like a magician who makes bread into flesh and wine into blood? That is why the worshippers of the devil imitate what we do, that is why they invert the sacraments as symbols of their rejection of God. Did Mylne not teach you that?"

I nodded. Inversion of the sacraments was a subject Duncan and I had touched on more than once.

Silvestri closed the box and put it back in the cupboard. When he returned to his seat, he seemed shrunken, troubled in spirit.

"I wish you to understand that, in showing you what I am about to, I take a very great risk. Duncan Mylne is well aware of my existence, but not even he knows just how much information I possess. You have been his subordinate. Even now, he is trying to find you and bring you back to his side. In confiding in you, I shall be placing my life in your hands. Is that a responsibility you are willing to accept?"

I hesitated.

"Surely you're better equipped than I am to protect yourself against Mylne. But if you mean, will I reveal anything I learn here to him, the simple answer is no. Not under any circumstances."

He looked sharply at me.

"Be very careful how you phrase things. 'Any circumstances' is a very broad promise to make. It would be unwise to underestimate Duncan Mylne. He is very dangerous indeed. I have outwitted and outmaneuvered him more than once, but I have yet to defeat him. His powers are considerable, and I could not guarantee that, in open conflict, he would not destroy me."

He stood, moving slowly and deliberately, and for a moment I could see pain swallow his eyes.

"Come with me," he said. "There are things I have to show you."

We followed him next door. This was a small but well-stocked library, the door to which was bolted and shut by a massive lock. I noticed that the windows were barred and that all the books were behind glass doors, each with a lock and strong bolts.

"I'm sorry if my security measures seem excessive," he said as we entered. "But I did not have all these locks installed merely for effect. There are books in here which no one may read without the express sanction of the church. I hope you understand. They are kept here by special dispensation and on very strict conditions."

He crossed to a locked cabinet in one corner and took out a bundle of dark blue files. When he was satisfied he had all he wanted, he relocked the cabinet and limped back to where Harriet and I were standing. We sat down at a small table in the center of the room and he switched on an overhead lamp. Opening the top file, he drew something from it and passed it to me.

It was a photograph of a man of about fifty, dressed in rather old-fashioned clothes, dating from the 1940s, as far as I could tell.

"Do you recognize him?" Father Silvestri asked.

I nodded.

"It's Duncan Mylne," I said. "Or his near double."

"That is his father, Stuart Mylne. The photograph was taken in 1943, in London. Now, what about this?"

He passed me a second photograph, this time of a man of about forty, dressed in the clothes of a late Victorian gentleman. Allowing for differences of age and style, this too greatly resembled Duncan.

"I take it this is his grandfather."

"You're perfectly right. That is Angus Mylne. He was born in Edinburgh in 1846 and died in 1908. His son Stuart was born in 1890 and died in 1961. Duncan was born in 1943 and is still living."

He paused and took the photographs from me, passing them to Harriet.

"Those," Father Silvestri continued, "are the basic facts concerning the last three generations of the Mylne family. Except that almost none of it is true. Angus certainly was born in 1846: I have seen the entry in the parish register for that year. I have also seen birth certificates for Stuart and Duncan. Angus did indeed set up the cloth export company which still bears the family name, and of which Duncan is now a nonexecutive director.

"But many years ago I began to grow suspicious about the Mylne history. I discovered quite by accident that Stuart Mylne, Duncan's father, lived in London between 1929 and 1940. He owned a house in Lowndes Square which was destroyed in the Blitz. He vanished soon after that, only to pop up here in Scotland again when Duncan was born in 1943.

"I heard unpleasant rumors about Mylne's time in London. There was, in particular, a story that, when the fire brigade went through the ruins of his house after the bombing, they discovered some rather gruesome things in the cellar. There was something of a scandal, but it was quickly hushed up: stories of that kind were reckoned to be bad for morale while the war was on.

"I thought there was something odd about the fact that all three Mylnes traveled as widely as they did, often staying away from home for years at a time. The more I asked around, the more I found that things did not fit together. In the end, I analyzed what I knew and discovered something very curious: no one seemed to have seen Angus Mylne with his son Stuart after the boy was about ten; and no one had ever seen Stuart with Duncan after about the same age. Stuart appears to have made his first appearance in public around the age of twenty, Duncan when he studied law at St. Andrews at the age of eighteen."

He paused.

"It is my firm belief," he went on "that Angus, Stuart, and Duncan Mylne are one and the same person. He has never died, and he means to go on living, reappearing every so often as his own son."

"Do you mean he is reborn in some way as a child?" asked Harriet.

Silvestri shook his head.

"No, I do not mean that. I am not speaking of reincarnation in any shape or form. Mylne is simply rejuvenated, if we may put it that way. The children will have been orphans procured for the purpose of registering the birth and lending substance to the imposture for a while. I fear they will have met their end as soon as they outlived their usefulness."

He went on to explain how Angus Mylne, devastated by the death of his first wife, Constance, took to the study of the magical arts. After years of getting nowhere, he stumbled on a book that seemed to offer him everything he sought.

"You've seen it," he said to me. "You have Angus's own copy with you in that briefcase."

"The *Matrix Aeternitatis*? But surely . . . "

I opened my briefcase and took out the copy of the *Matrix* . Silvestri took it from me and opened it at the flyleaf. Rummaging in his files, he found an old letter.

"That's Angus Mylne's signature at the bottom," he said. He passed both book and letter to me. I compared the signature on the flyleaf with that at the foot of the letter. They were by one and the same hand.

"On the strength of what he read in this book," Silvestri continued, "Angus Mylne traveled to Morocco. He went there ostensibly to engage in trade, but in reality it was to seek help in his studies. He spent seven years there, and found what he was looking for in the person of an occult master in Fez. From this man he learned how to defy death, and it's said he continues to visit him each year in order to deepen his knowledge and to take whatever action is necessary to prevent his own death."

"Sheikh Ahmad," I whispered.

"Precisely. An old man then, and much older now. It's also reported that, on returning from Africa, Mylne spent a year and more locked in his private rooms at Penshiel House, along with the remains of his wife, trying to bring her back to life. Whether he succeeded or not isn't clear."

I shuddered. I had read the chapters in the *Matrix* devoted to the resurrection of corpses, and very unpleasant they had been. It was all too easy to imagine Angus Mylne shut up in a room somewhere with his wife's corpse, willing her to return, performing again and again the rituals he hoped would bring her back to life.

"What about Duncan?" I asked. "If he was really his father grown young again, didn't anyone find the resemblance strange?"

"Why should they? Anyone who had known his father in the old days would believe he was dead and that Duncan was his double. That would not seem strange in a child. He arrived in

Edinburgh in the 1960s, and stayed on in order to practice law. He had a large private income, so it wasn't hard for him to make his way to the top. And there wasn't just money—he also possessed age, experience, and the benefit of more years spent in study than his contemporaries had lived. He'd attended trials that were only known to his friends from the pages of books.

"Not long after he was called to the bar, he started to spend time with some of the occult groups that were thriving here then. I think he'd already set up a circle of his own in London, and it was no trouble to transfer most of its activities to the north. He'd begun to make recruits inside groups like the Fraternity of the Old Path—as I think you already know. You weren't by any means the first, but I pray you may prove the last."

He paused.

"There's something else you should know," he said. "One of the people who became closely involved with Mylne and his circle was a bookseller called Clement Markham. Markham was an Englishman who'd moved to Edinburgh in the fifties. He ran a secondhand and antiquarian business from a shop somewhere in the Haymarket district.

"Around 1975, the shop was raided by the obscene publications squad, who'd been given a tip-off that Markham was handling pornography on the side.

"I don't know whether they ever found any dirty books, but they did come across the bodies of three small children. Markham was arrested and tried, and in the course of the trial it was suggested that the children had met their fate as sacrifices in rituals conducted by Markham.

"His connection with Mylne came out, of course, but there was never anything to tie the eminent young advocate to the murders, and nothing ever came out in court. No doubt Mylne was able to use his influence to make sure his name was kept out of the investigation. All the same, people did talk, and since then Mylne has enjoyed a poor reputation in certain circles. Markham died in prison in 1981. His bookshop has remained empty ever since."

"Not quite empty," I said. My voice sounded hollow to me. I was shivering inside.

While we had been talking, Harriet had been studying the photographs of Mylne, both those that I had looked at and the others in Silvestri's thick file. In the silence that followed my remark, she picked one out and looked at it for a short time.

"Look at this, Andrew," she said. "It shows Angus Mylne with his wife, Constance—the one he's supposed to have tried to bring back to life. How horrible, spending a year shut up with her corpse. Here, take a look."

I took the photograph from her and glanced at it, first at Mylne, then at his wife. As I did so, the photograph fell from my hand. I felt myself grow giddy. The room seemed to flash in and out, and I wanted to retch.

"What is it, Andrew? What's the matter?" Harriet got up from her chair and put a hand on my arm. Silvestri frowned.

I took several deep breaths. Slowly, I came to myself and was able to sit up straight.

"What happened, Andrew? You look terrible."

I pointed numbly at the photograph. It stared up at me.

"She's Catriona's double," I said. "Now I know why he had her remains removed from their grave. He failed once—now he's trying again.'

Chapter

30

WE STAYED WITH SILVESTRI until about three o'clock.

"I'd like you both to come back this evening," he said as we were leaving. "There are some enquiries I have to make. What you have told me has been extremely useful. But you must not forget that you are both in mortal danger. You, Andrew, in particular. You have crossed Mylne, and he does not forgive easily. At the moment, you are useful to him, but once you have outlived that usefulness he will not hesitate to destroy you."

"I know this may sound stupid," I said, "but is there any point in our going to the police with what we know?"

Silvestri thought it over.

"It's not entirely foolish," he said. "In spite of his powers, Duncan Mylne is still a human being.

Public disgrace would be immensely difficult for him. Imprisonment would be a very real threat to his continued existence, if it stopped him visiting Morocco and having access to the books and papers he needs. He depends greatly on his personal wealth; a poor man could not achieve what he has done. He needs the freedom and the ability to travel, to buy rare books, to keep his church and his home in the country.

"But the police will not dare to move against him unless they have cast-iron proof. You may succeed in getting his associates arrested, as happened to Markham, but Mylne himself is certain to prove more difficult to pin down."

"If we found the child . . . Or Catriona's remains . . . Cameron would be bound to act. And Duncan couldn't wriggle out of it."

"Don't be so sure. But let me think all this over and speak with one or two other people. You are not alone in this struggle."

He embraced us in turn, in the awkward manner of someone whose normal intercourse with others is guarded.

"God bless you," he said. "And protect you."

WE TOOK A BUS BACK TO TOWN. Harriet wanted to get back to Dean Village, but I was still worried about my father. There was just time to keep my appointment with Ramsey McLean.

"You go on," I said. "I won't be very long—he'll have patients to see. But I would like his opinion on Father's condition."

"I'll wait for you. Don't be too late; we can eat before going back to Silvestri's."

MCLEAN WAS WAITING for me as arranged. It felt good to see him, as though he could put everything right again as he had done when I was a sick child. He shook hands warmly and asked me to sit down.

"I'll sit here," he said, perching himself on the edge of the examination couch. "We're old friends, I hardly think a desk is necessary."

"I hope this isn't inconvenient."

"Not at all. I was worried, to tell you the truth, when you said your father was ill. I haven't heard from him in months. Of course, he's never been a well man, though he's kept it well hidden. I take it it's his heart at last."

"I wasn't aware . . . "

"No, of course you weren't. I told you, he kept it well hidden."

"The thing is, it's not his heart at all, as far as I know."

His eyebrows shot up.

"Is it not? Just tell me what you know and I'll see if I can make sense of it."

I described my father's symptoms as best I could, and from them moved on to Iain and how he had died. McLean listened patiently to me, nodding from time to time, or grunting.

"And you think your father has developed the same mysterious condition?"

"It's not that simple," I said.

"Oh?" The eyebrows went up again. I began to

explain as best I could, beginning with the double desecration of Catriona's grave as the most tangible of the matters connected with what I believed to be happening. He listened without comment or interruption of any kind, still nodding or making encouraging noises at suitable points.

I showed him Iain's letter and told him all that Silvestri had said, without revealing the priest's name.

"I saw the photographs myself," I said. "There was no mistake—not about Mylne, not about Catriona. I'd swear to both."

"I'm sure," he said, and went back to the letter. He read it through a second time carefully, and when he finally put it down he seemed troubled. I could hear the sounds of people moving in the corridors outside. The afternoon surgery had begun.

McLean slipped off the couch and resumed his seat behind the desk. Without a word to me, he picked up the telephone.

"Miss Menzies, could you see that no one disturbs me for the next half hour? Yes, I know it's packed, but I have important business to discuss and I can't be interrupted. Send anyone home who doesn't seem urgent, and ask Dr. Melrose to deal with the rest."

He put down the receiver and looked across the desk at me.

"Well, Andrew, you seem to have got yourself in one hell of a mess."

"You believe me, then?"

He snorted and shook his head.

"If you mean, do I believe all this stuff about

magicians and bringing people back from the dead, of course I don't. I'm a man of science, or I like to pretend I am. But I'm perfectly willing to believe that something unpleasant is going on. There are cranks enough in this city to fill a dozen asylums. This man Mylne sounds like a very nasty bit of work. I'm surprised he wasn't locked away years ago.

"Unfortunately, I think you will have your work cut out to prove anything against him. I agree that he is a likely culprit in the business of Catriona's grave and the murder of the infant that was found there. It is possible that he has some sort of delusion about being identical with his father and grandfather, and that he may be acting the delusion out.

"The occult business you can rule out. From what you say, you were given a cocktail of drugs while in Morocco, and these will have given you hallucinations and disturbed dreams. You saw an old man there and thought he was dead."

"But I saw him."

"You saw him sleeping. Believe me, Andrew, it is far from impossible to enter a comatose state in which sleep appears very like death. There are drugs that can produce a similar effect."

"What about the noises?"

"If you are in half as disturbed a state as you were when I last saw you, I would not be at all surprised that you were hearing things again."

"But Harriet—she heard them as well."

"Yes, I am sure. But I should very much like to speak with her about what she did hear. You are overwrought, she is a recent widow and probably quite on edge herself. Look, Andrew, I'm not trying to rubbish what you have told me, simply to shed some rational light on it. You're a trained academic, you know the value of an objective assessment of the facts.

"I think you are perfectly right to be concerned about Mylne and any associates he may have. The priest's evidence may be worthless as far as all this superstitious twaddle goes, but for all that he may be able to provide reasonable grounds for the police to act on."

"What about the photographs? Don't you think they prove that the three Mylnes are really one person?"

He laughed gently and shook his head.

"No doubt there is a resemblance; but no more than one might expect to find between three generations of the same family. Believe me, Andrew, you are letting your irrational fears blind you to what is obvious to anyone else. It will do you no harm to take a mild sedative and to drink some more of that herbal remedy I gave you before. I'll have some made up for you to take home."

"Is there nothing you can do about my father?"

"I can make no promises. I'll do what I can. If your friend Mrs. Gillespie will allow it, I'd like to see the Royal Infirmary's records on her husband. I'll ask Boyd what he can tell me about your father, and I'll monitor the case. At the very least I should be able to set your mind at rest."

"So you don't think my father has the same condition that killed Iain?"

"I don't know that yet. The symptoms do sound remarkably similar and a little unusual in both cases, but I'd rather defer judgment until I have harder facts."

"What about Mylne? Can you help us do something about him?"

He pondered before answering.

"Really, Andrew, it isn't my province. It will take a proper police enquiry to establish any guilt. But your prima facie evidence is interesting, if not convincing. I think you were right not to tell the police your suspicions on Saturday. They would not have believed a word. But there may be enough here to get them moving. Do you mind if I keep your friend's letter? I'd like to reread it this evening and make one or two enquiries of my own.

"As for yourself, my advice is to go home now, take two of the tablets I'm going to give you, and get some rest. Will you do that?"

I nodded.

"Good man. It's time we got you properly on your feet. If it's at all possible, you should consider going to Stornoway for a few months. But let's wait until we know what the news is about your father."

He gave me a small packet of tranquilizers and told the nurse to give me a large bottle of the herbal medicine I had had before.

"This is slower acting," he said, "but it will have greater benefits in the long run, and no side effects. I don't want you getting addicted to the tranquilizers. Take a tablespoon before meals. Make sure you have some with whatever you eat when you get in. And I'd like to see you tomorrow, if that's all right."

"I'll make an appointment on the way out."

He shook his head.

"No, I'd rather you stayed at home for a few days. From the sound of it, you've been overdoing things. That isn't good in your condition. I'd like you to stay in this evening and get an early night. Take one of those tablets at bedtime, it should help you sleep. I'll call in the morning on my rounds. Are you still in the same flat?"

"No, I've moved." I was about to give him my new address when I remembered that I had arranged to stay with Harriet. "I'm going to be with Harriet over the next few days," I said. "You'd better have her address." I wrote it down and left it on the desk.

As I reached the door, I turned and asked a question that had been bothering me all afternoon.

"You don't think Catriona's body is in that church, do you? Would he have taken her there?"

He shrugged.

"I really don't know, Andrew. But we can get the police onto it and, if she has been taken there, they'll find her and have her returned to Glasgow. For God's sake, don't even think of poking about in there yourself."

Chapter
31

HARRIET WAS WAITING WHEN I got to Dean Village. She had prepared a meal, tiger prawns cooked in white wine.

"I wanted to do a little better than last night," she said. "We should eat soon. Silvestri rang to say he's expecting us at seven. We can get a taxi."

"Harriet," I said, "I'm sorry, but I can't go tonight. I promised Dr. McLean I'd stay in. He's given me some stuff to help me sleep, and he wants me to have an early night. If he says it's all right in the morning, I'll go over with you again then."

She frowned.

"Silvestri said he wanted to see both of us. He needs to speak to you." She shrugged. "Well, I suppose it can't be helped. McLean's right, you do look tired out. An early night will do you good. Look, I have to pick up my car from outside your place. Is there anything you need me to bring back?"

"I don't think you should go there on your own."

"I'll be all right. None of these manifestations start till late at night, you said."

"No, but—"

"I'll be in and out. Make a note of what you need. I'll pop over soon."

While Harriet served the meal, I took my medicine. It tasted more bitter than I remembered. While we ate I told her about the talk I'd with McLean.

"He's being very rational about it all," I said, "but maybe that's just what we need at the moment."

She shook her head.

"It still leaves too many things unanswered. Last night was no hallucination. We heard what we did. None of this can be explained away, Andrew, and I think it could be dangerous to try."

She sipped from her wine glass.

"By the way," she went on, "Silvestri wanted to know how you came into contact with Mylne. He seemed to think it was important."

"I met him at the Fraternity of the Old Path. There's nothing mysterious about that. Iain seemed to think that was how Mylne made contact with all his potential recruits."

"Okay, I'll tell him that. I'll drive over and explain to him that you'll try to get over in the morning. Or maybe he can come here."

"I'm sorry I can't make it tonight. But I really don't feel up to it."

"Don't worry. He'll understand."

I made the note of things I needed from my flat, and explained where they would be.

"Do you mind if I use your phone to ring my mother?" I asked. "I promised I'd ring her every night. She'll worry if I don't get in touch."

"Of course, you know you're free to use anything you like. I won't be long."

"I'll wait for you."

"No, go to bed if you're tired. The guest room's been made up. I'll see you in the morning."

After she had gone, I felt restless. I sat reading for a while, picking books at random from the shelves, but I could not concentrate. Tired though I was, I was still too wound up to think of sleep. To fill in the time until Harriet returned, I switched on the television, just in time to catch the local news.

A baby had been taken from its pram in Gilmerton, on the outskirts of Edinburgh. There were, as yet, no suspects, but the police had not ruled out a connection with a similar case in Glasgow. I went to the bathroom and threw up the meal I had just eaten.

I did not like being in the house on my own. The silence preyed on my nerves, intensifying even the smallest sound until I was ready to jump at anything. Why did Harriet not return? I fretted, knowing I should never have allowed her to go to Drumdryan Street on her own.

Desperate to speak to someone, I made my call to Stornoway. My father had made a slight improvement, but Dr. Boyd still insisted on having the tests done in Inverness. They would probably fly my father there in the morning, provided he had not suffered a relapse.

"Ramsey McLean will probably be in touch," I said.

"That's kind of him. He'll have been wondering about your father."

"Why's that?" I asked. "I only spoke to him about it today."

"Oh, your father rang him about a week ago, when he was planning to visit you. He was thinking of staying with Ramsey, if there was room."

"I don't understand," I said. "He said nothing to me today about speaking to you."

"He must have forgotten. Did he say if he has any idea what may be wrong?"

"What? No, no, he wants to speak with Boyd first. You know doctors, they'll never commit themselves."

"That's true enough. I have terrible trouble getting Boyd even to admit there's something wrong."

"Mother, I have to go. If you do go to Inverness tomorrow, will you let me know? I'm staying with Harriet Gillespie for a few days. You can ring me here."

"Is something wrong? You're not ill yourself, are you?"

"Just a bit tired."

"Have you been overdoing it again?"

"A little bit. But I'm in good hands. Ramsey's given me some medicine like before."

I gave her Harriet's number and rang off.

Why had McLean not mentioned his conversation with my mother? It would have been the most natural thing to say something like, "I spoke to your father only last week. He was thinking of coming to Edinburgh for a visit." But that was not what he had said. I remembered now. What he had said was, "I haven't heard from him in months."

That was not all I remembered. My first thought, when asked how I had met Duncan Mylne, had been of our brushes at the meetings of the Fraternity. But we had only met properly that day at the pub, when he had come to my table as though by appointment. And I now remembered who had arranged for me to be there. Ramsey McLean.

The doorbell rang. I sighed with relief. Harriet must have forgotten her keys. I could not have sat there much longer, a prey to mounting fear.

I got up and went to the door. Harriet and I had to talk. I was starting to let things get out of proportion. Perhaps I was growing paranoid, finding everyone around me somehow sinister, part of a plot.

I opened the door. Ramsey McLean was standing on the step.

"Good evening, Andrew. I hope I'm not disturbing you."

"No, I . . . I was just watching television."

"Do you mind if I come in?"

"No, no . . . Of course not."

He stepped forward into the hall. As he did so, there was a soft movement behind him. A second figure stepped forward, moving into the light.

"Hello, Andrew," he said. It was Duncan Mylne. He had not changed. "It's time we had a little chat."

Chapter
32

AT FIRST, THERE WAS ONLY SILENCE. And if I opened my eyes, there was darkness; it did not alter, however long I stared. I thought I had gone blind. Perhaps McLean's medicine had done this to me, turned me blind and deaf. But I could not remember clearly. I did recall his arrival at the door, then Mylne's appearance, and being forced back into the house; but after that my memory was a blank. I had no idea where I was, or how I had come to be there.

The blackness and the silence just went on and on, as though locked inside my head. I shut my eyes and clasped my arms round my body. I could feel, at least, and I could tell that I was bitterly cold. I do not know how long I sat huddled like that, shivering, blind, conscious of nothing but the cold air and the discomfort of the stone on which I sat.

As my head cleared, so I became gradually more aware of my surroundings. I could hear sounds, ugly sounds that I wanted to shut out again the moment I heard them. Things slithering. Things bumping. Things sucking.

I opened my eyes. It was still pitch dark. But I guessed where I had been taken.

Voices nearby, whispering, then fading again. The sound of footsteps advancing, then receding. In their absence, the other sounds returned, louder than ever. A sound like bone scraping across a stone floor. The slithering again. And that obscene flapping sound I had heard so often before. I put my hands over my ears and shut my eyes. It did little good. I knew they were there.

"Andrew, how are you feeling now?"

It was McLean, his voice solicitous, as though he had come to visit an ailing patient. I opened my eyes and blinked hard. He was standing next to me holding a lantern of some kind.

"I'm sorry if you have been uncomfortable, Andrew, but you must understand that it is for the best. I think you must have taken rather too large a dose of my medicine. But the effects will wear off soon.

"Angus is upstairs. He'll be ready to start as soon as the preparations are completed and you are feeling more yourself. You mustn't worry, he doesn't intend to let anything unpleasant happen to you. Quite the contrary. If you cooperate, you'll find him most appreciative. He has a great affection for you, and profound admiration. Believe me, he would not see you suffer for anything.

"But you must also realize that he is impatient. He has waited over a century for this moment. And your recent ingratitude has not pleased him. If you remain uncooperative, he could well grow angry. I advise you to avoid that at all costs. He'll take you through the ritual until you've got it right. You're already familiar with most of it, the rest can be read directly from the *Matrix*. The main thing is to be relaxed. I'll give you something just before you begin, something to calm your nerves."

To my surprise, I found that I could speak. I had feared that the power of speech might have been snatched from me.

"What if I don't do what he wants?"

"That would be extremely foolhardy. Don't even think of it. If you make him happy, your father will experience a full recovery. Otherwise, his condition will deteriorate. It is really that simple. The pain can be extended almost indefinitely. Your mother is not immune. If you won't have pity on yourself, at least think of them. What is he asking, after all?"

"Catriona is not his wife."

"Do you think that matters to a man like him? He wants her. He deserves to have her."

"She won't want him."

"Do you imagine he hasn't thought of that? You are really being very naive. If he can bring her back from the dead, don't you think he can influence her affections at the same time?"

"Then why does he need me? Why can't he do it himself?"

"Tell me, Andrew—would you like him to try?

Without your presence and your participation, the whole thing may go wrong again."

He hesitated, as though reaching a difficult decision.

"Andrew, there is something I think you should see."

Bending down, he took my arm and helped me to my feet. I felt giddy, my limbs were stiff with cold. Standing, I could see more clearly, though mercifully the low light of the lantern left much in shadow.

We were in a low-ceilinged crypt, in a long stone-walled room lined with coffins. McLean urged me forward. As I walked, I saw them on all sides, nearly two centuries of decay lined against the walls or crammed into niches. Heavy cobwebs hung down in tattered sheets, draping enormous studded boxes and narrow wooden chests, piled higgledy-piggledy on top of one another.

Here and there, a stack had fallen, the weight of succeeding generations too great for those who lay underneath. Lids had cracked open, side had collapsed, entire coffins had split open, spilling their contents onto the pavement. Great spiders almost as large as mice scuttled between the cracks.

But it was not the sight of so much decay that troubled me most. It was the sounds that came from the closed boxes as we passed. He had been coming here for years, practising, honing his necromantic skills, making his mistakes. And the mistakes were still here.

Something was banging and scraping against its coffin lid. I hurried past.

"They can hear us," said McLean. Even in the unnatural light I could tell that his ordinarily ruddy face was white. "We disturb them. We remind them."

We crossed through some vaulting and came into a separate room, much smaller than the one we had just left. The smell of decay was, curiously, stronger here, yet masked in part by another, darker, smell.

In a niche set in the rear wall stood a large Victorian coffin with a bowed lid. The doctor half steered, half pushed me toward it. Close by, the dark smell was overpowering. McLean set down the lantern on a low shelf and let go of my arm. I did not think of running. I had nowhere to run to. With both hands, he pushed the heavy lid aside far enough to allow me to see inside. I saw him avert his own face as he brought the lamp closer and pushed me forward. The smell that rose up from inside was almost more than I could bear. I thought I would pass out again.

I looked down. How I wish I had instead taken my chances and fled. The memory of that one fractured glance will not leave me, I have it in me at all times, it will remain there until I die. Perhaps it will not leave me even then. For there is no paradise, I know there is not, I knew it at that moment.

The thing in the coffin wore a long Victorian dress. I remembered where I had seen the dress before—in the photograph of Angus Mylne and his wife, Constance. And I remembered something else. The thing I had seen on the snowy meadow at Penshiel House, crawling and stumbling through the moonlight, as though blind.

I gasped and turned my head away. But not before I had seen one last abominable detail. The thing that had once been Constance Mylne had neither nose nor mouth, nor even jaw, but it was still breathing.

McLean closed the coffin. We staggered out of the fetid little chamber. The warning could not have been clearer. I thought of Catriona, and I thought of what I had just seen in the coffin; Angus Mylne had given me no choice.

We walked back to where we had started. Things moved in the shadows. I tried not to look.

"I'll leave you now," said McLean. "For a little while. To think things over."

"Please," I said. "Don't leave me down here in the dark."

"You'll find the dark is preferable to light, Andrew. There are things here it is better not to see. I won't leave you long, I promise."

He turned and walked away, and moments later I was in the pitch dark again. But this time I knew exactly where I was and what surrounded me. They did not stop their rustling and scraping. And I did not dare put my hands over my ears for fear they came too close.

Chapter
33

I CANNOT BE SURE HOW MUCH time passed. Minutes?
Hours? It really does not matter. Time was not
important down there. A minute could seem like an
eternity. All that counted was not being there.

There was a movement in the shadows to my
right, then a light. Startled, I looked round. An old
man came shuffling toward me, supported by
McLean. The doctor held a lantern as before, and
the other man a candle in a holder. It was impossible to tell how old he was. His face and body were
skeletal, as though he had been brought up from
one of the coffins underneath. He wore a long black
gown of pure silk, and leaned on a tall staff. Strands
of long white hair clung to an otherwise naked
skull. Had it not been for two bright eyes in the
sockets, I would have thought him dead.

"I have missed you, Andrew," he said. The voice was thin, barely recognizable. "You were an intelligent companion. You had promise. I could have made something of you, but you let yourself be distracted by sentiment. I promised you the mastery you sought, and you still betrayed me. It is a great disappointment. I expected greater things from you."

"I didn't betray you," I said. "You betrayed yourself years ago, you tried to have something no one has a right to."

"Eternal life? Is that what you mean? Don't be so ridiculous. That's hardly what this is all about. Eternal life on its own is grotesque. It has no greater value or attraction than life on its own. Ask anyone. Do they want bare life, mere existence? I don't think so. What they all want is life together with those things that make it worthwhile: money, pleasure, good health, love, excitement, knowledge, contentment, success, power, children—the list is as variable as human nature. We can't have everything, that's something we learn early on, most of us. But we take what we can get, and we go on hoping that there may be something more, something we don't have but can reasonably expect.

"Continued life without these things would be merely a prolongation of misery. Given the vicissitudes of our physical existence, it would be unreasonable not to anticipate some setbacks: disease, disablement, a decline in one's fortunes, the loss of dear ones . . . Under such circumstances, prolonged existence would quickly become intolerable. From seeking life, we would rush to welcome death.

"No, Andrew, if there is to be life eternal, there must be the means to ensure that one remains protected from these vicissitudes. It pays to be circumspect. The same magic that can grant life can also bestow good fortune in the shape of power and wealth and physical well-being. Some have attained one, some the other; but it has only been granted to a small elite of men to achieve both together."

He paused. While he had been speaking, I had seen that more than youth had been stripped away. All the politeness, all the bonhomie had gone. In their place I saw nothing but an iron will, the single-minded determination of a man who seeks only his own ends.

"Dr. McLean has shown you some of what we keep down here. You have had time to think about what is waiting if you are uncooperative. But before we go upstairs, there is something else I want you to see."

McLean took my arm and urged me forward. We went through a low arch, then another, and came up against a wooden door with large rusted hinges. The doctor bent forward and turned a key in the lock. The door opened onto pitch darkness.

We did not enter. McLean stood beside me and shone his light inside. I could see very little. Just the hard shapes of coffins, and a brightness of bones, and then, slow and confusing, crawling white forms, and the sound of sucking and nibbling. I remembered the woodcut in the book that lay open on the lid of the coffin. And I thought of the words at the end of Iain's letter: *Destroy everything They are swarming Angus brought them back from Morocco*

I closed my eyes. Mylne's voice came out of the darkness behind me, liquid and emotionless.

"The Carthaginians called them Ibad-Tanit, the servants of Tanit. The Arabs simply called them *didan*, maggots. They were found in an underground chamber in Tangier. You have been there with the comte d'Hervilly. The Carthaginians found it and called it Mikdash Tanit: the Temple of Tanit. She was their goddess of eternal life. But more than that, she granted power to those who worshiped her. And she continues to grant power."

McLean withdrew the lamp. I could see only darkness now, but I could hear the servants of Tanit as they ate.

"It's time to finish what we came here for," said Mylne. McLean closed the door and locked it. Mylne took my arm and guided me to a flight of narrow stairs.

WE CLIMBED SLOWLY and came out into the main body of the church. The old, dark church of my worst dreams. As before, the only light came from candles set on tall sconces in the aisles. I had thought there would be others waiting, but the body of the church was empty. There were to be just the three of us for this ceremony.

In the chancel, where the altar had once stood, a trestle held a coffin. At each corner stood a candlestick and a burning candle. The last time I had seen it had been in the cemetery in Glasgow, when they lowered Catriona to what I had thought would be her final resting place. The lid had been prized off and replaced loosely on top.

And so my last instruction began. Mylne sat down with me and rehearsed me in what I should say and do. There were to be two rituals, and I understood why he was there that night as an old man. The time had come for another transformation, and for that he needed me. Not my body, but the life in it. He would suck me dry like someone sucking juice from a pomegranate, and discard the husk. Duncan Mylne would move from Edinburgh and, after a discreet interval, his son would appear in London or Paris or wherever took his fancy, a young man of intelligence and promise, with a young and beautiful wife.

It was well into the morning before he was satisfied. My wording was perfect, my gestures accurate. All that remained was to put them together, beginning with the ritual to bring Catriona back among the living.

We stood in front of the coffin. Mylne began in a loud voice, invoking powers I had not even heard of, the names of deities and forces as old as death itself. This went on for some time. Out of the corner of my eye, I could see something moving in the shadows formed by the choir stalls. I looked more closely and saw a huddle of white shapes, squirming and throbbing like a pack of rats. The servants of Tanit.

Mylne's voice faded and he turned to me.

"Now, Andrew. It is time to begin."

I started to speak, reciting the words of the ritual almost by heart, glancing down from time to time at the open pages of the book. Mylne had a second copy, with which he followed me carefully, to ensure that all was done according to the text.

The *Kalibool Kolood* is divided into fourteen chapters or *abwab*, each subdivided into seven sections known as *fusul*. Each of these *fusul* is devoted to a separate aspect of the topic under discussion, with the spells arranged in the last three *fusul* of each *bab*. In addition, Mylne had added his own incantations on the basis of emendations by Sheikh Ahmad. These he passed to me at the appropriate times, and after reading them I would return to the original text.

It was as we reached the seventh *fasl* of the fifth *bab* that I became aware of a soft, irregular noise. As I reached the end of the incantation, there was a silence in which I listened carefully. A dull banging was coming from inside Catriona's coffin.

Mylne held my arm more tightly.

"Go on," he urged. "Do not break off now."

I continued, though my hand shook and my voice trembled. The knocking inside the coffin grew louder. I remembered the thing I had seen in Constance Mylne's coffin in that room in the crypt, and I prayed for strength to go on. To my horror, the banging slowed and was replaced by a long, piercing cry that changed in moments to whimpering. It was not the crying of a woman, I realized, but the frightened cry of a small baby. And it too was coming from within the coffin.

"Go on," said Mylne.

I continued, lifting my voice so that it would cover the knocking and the crying. But I could recite neither quickly enough nor loudly enough to drown them out completely.

Suddenly, the candles around the coffin flickered. Something had disturbed the air. I heard a banging sound behind me, and the candles flickered wildly again. Beside me, Mylne had turned and was staring back down the nave. McLean did the same. And then I heard a man's voice calling my name.

"Andrew! Leave them and come to me."

I turned and looked into the shadows at the back of the church. Two figures stood in front of the door.

"It's all right, Andrew. Do as he says."

This was Harriet's voice, tense and full of fear, yet held steady in order to reassure me. The figures walked down the aisle, and I saw that Harriet had brought Father Silvestri.

Mylne pulled himself to his full height and pointed a finger at Silvestri.

"Get out of here, priest! There's nothing you can do."

Silvestri ignored him. He continued walking toward the chancel, speaking to me in a calm, quiet voice.

"He has no further hold over you, Andrew. Just step away from him. Go with Harriet. She knows what to do."

I started to step back, but at that moment the baby cried again. I could not leave it.

"Stay where you are, Andrew." Mylne's voice was cold and peremptory. "Ramsey, hold him fast."

McLean made to take my arm, but I was awake now and full of anger. I hit him full in the stomach and, as he doubled over, punched him hard in the throat. He fell back, choking and gasping for breath.

I stumbled forward to the coffin and pushed aside the lid. Dear God, I do not like to think of that moment. I did not want to look inside, yet I had to find the baby. It was lying against Catriona's breast. I picked it up and clutched it to me, then staggered backward.

At that moment I felt another arm take mine. Just as I was about to tear myself away, a voice whispered in my ear. A very gentle and familiar voice.

"Come with me, love. It's time for you to leave."

And I knew beyond all doubt that this was no simulacrum, that Catriona herself had found me.

She guided me through the confusion of the chancel, past flapping, shuffling shapes I dared not pause to examine, to where Silvestri and Harriet were waiting. I felt a kiss against my cheek, then she was gone.

Harriet reached forward and took the baby from me.

"My car's outside, Andrew. Let's get out of here."

I stammered.

"Catriona . . . "

Harriet nodded.

"Yes, I saw her. But you have to let her go."

The baby whimpered. Behind me, I heard Mylne's voice lifting in a conjuration. The candles flickered and went out.

Harriet pulled me to the door.

"What about Silvestri?" I asked.

"It's what he wants," said Harriet. "He knows what he's doing."

I turned at the open door. A bright, unnatural light was shining in the chancel. Angus Mylne stood against it, outlined, his arms held high above his head. I could hear his voice ringing through the empty building. A second figure, no more than a shadow, moved toward him as though fighting against a high wind.

"There's nothing more you can do," said Harriet.

I looked for the last time. Silvestri kept on moving. I could just make out his voice, low yet firm. The door closed and we were outside in the freezing cold.

Chapter

34

A YOUNG PRIEST WAS WAITING for us at the rectory. Silvestri had given him careful instructions on what to do with us.

"You must leave Edinburgh tonight," he said. "Both of you. I have some money you can take. You must never come back here, and no one must know where you have gone. You'll have to change your names, take on new identities. I will be able to help you.

"Andrew," he said, "I do not think you will ever know peace again until you die. That creature in Fez has long tentacles. Mylne is not easily tired, and he has a long memory. Wherever you go, you will have to be on the watch all the time. Trust no one, confide in no one, befriend no one, above all, let no one befriend you.

"Leave the baby with me tonight. I'll see it's taken care of and returned to its parents in the morning. There's nothing more you can do here."

Harriet had already got things together. She and the priest had gone to my flat and packed enough clothes for the journey.

"How did you know where to find me?" I asked.

"It was either there or Penshiel House," explained Harriet. "Silvestri was almost certain it would be the church, that that was where Catriona's remains were being kept."

"What will happen to them?"

The priest answered.

"I'll see the police are informed. And I'll make sure they don't come after you. Inspector Cameron's a Catholic: he'll understand."

"And Silvestri?" I asked. "We can't just leave him there."

"He is my responsibility," said the priest. "You have to think about yourself and Harriet."

We left soon afterward, driving north in Harriet's car. We drove on through the night, into greater and greater darkness. And on my cheek I could still feel the touch of lips that had not been there.

THE SEA INHABITS OUR DARKNESS and our light. Its rising and falling is a token that all is well, day by day. We live in a small house near an inlet on a small island that I shall not name. Harriet weaves and takes in local children from time to time, to help them with their English. I have learned the art of dry-stone walling and am a passable mason. From time to time, I write articles for academic journals, but not often. It helps that I speak Gaelic here. People do not ask too many questions.

My father died six months after we left Edinburgh. I saw his obituary in the local paper. My mother lives alone. I telephone her every week, but I cannot tell her where I live now.

Father Enzio Silvestri was buried in private in a Jesuit cemetery in Florence. The circumstances of his death were never made public. I pray for him each night, though I do not believe.

Harriet and I were married soon after we arrived here; it seemed best, and we find we love one another well. We both have memories, we are both restless, but we are learning contentment. The sea is vast, and cruel in winter. Harriet expects a child next spring.

I HEARD SOMETHING OUTSIDE the house last night. Perhaps it was just my imagination. I said nothing to Harriet. But if it returns tonight, I will have to tell her. It will be time for us to move again.

For us it has become as the words of the Psalm:

> 'S an fhàsach air seachran chaidh
> an ionad falamh f às;
> Is bail' air bith cha d'fhuaradh leo
> gu còmhnuidh ann no tàmh.

They wandered in the wilderness in a solitary way; they found no city to dwell in.

Jonathan Aycliffe is a pseudonym for Daniel Easterman, the best-selling author of NAME OF THE BEAST, THE JUDAS TESTAMENT, BROTHERHOOD OF THE TOMB, THE NINTH BUDDHA, and other thrillers. He was born in Ireland in 1949 and studied English, Persian, and Arabic at the Universities of Dublin, Edinburgh, and Cambridge. For several years he was a professor at Newcastle University. He currently lives in England with his wife.